THE GOLDEN GALARNEAUS

THE GOLDEN GALARNEAUS
Jacques Godbout

Translated by Patricia Claxton

Coach House Press
Toronto

Published with the assistance of the Canada Council,
the Department of Canadian Heritage, the Ontario Arts Council
and the Ontario Publishing Centre.

Coach House Press
760 Bathurst Street, 2nd floor
Toronto, Canada M5S 2R6

FIRST EDITION
1 3 5 7 9 8 6 4 2
Printed in Canada

Canadian Cataloguing in Publication Data
Godbout, Jacques, 1933–
[Temps des Galarneau. English]
The golden Galarneaus
Translation of: Le temps des Galarneau.
ISBN 0-88910-487-5

I. Title. II. Title: Le temps des Galarneau.
English.

PS8513.036T13 1995   C843'.54   C95-931945-X
PQ3919.2.G63T413 1995

For Anni and Jean-Marie B.
in deepest friendship,

—J.G.

I wonder if anybody will ever ask me, "Galarneau, what were things like in your time?" In my time!

—*Hail Galarneau!* (page 28)

1. It's kind of severe. Polished black shoes with crêpe rubber soles, blue shirt (pale, autumn-sky blue), wool socks, a regulation tie that goes with the serge suit, which is royal blue and has plastic imitation-pearl buttons (a double row on each cuff, big as silver dollars) and at the shoulder the company logo: the planet Earth crossed with a gold lightning bolt.

It suits me fine. The first time I put it on I thought I'd look silly in it. I didn't! It made me look good, suited me to a T. The rest of them at work can't all say that for themselves. Especially Jean-Charles whose belly hangs out over his pants. Still, you have to make allowances for Jean-Charles, he's old, been there since long before Harry Sécurité expanded. That's the company founded fifteen years ago by Harry Rosen, who owned four yardgoods stores. These days yardgoods are sold by the metre. Everything changes, not always for the better. We can't even tell the same jokes we used to, like the one that made Papa roar with laughter when he opened the paper and read about the annual clearance of whitestuffs by the yard at Madame Lalongé's: *"Madame Lalongé annonce son écoulement annuel de blanc à la verge."* Papa cut that one out and sent it to *Le Canard enchaîné* in Paris, France's answer to *National Lampoon*, and got a year's free subscription for it. They reproduced it with comments (which I'll leave to the imagination) on Madame Lalongé, maple syrup and the sexual practices of the Québécois.

Well. This was the period when there was a pretty fuzzy

line between English and French. In those days Monsieur Rosen would have called his agency "Harry's Security", no doubt about it. English was more serious than French, better for scaring off two-bit shoplifters. Nowadays nothing scares people any more. Not that they're braver than they used to be, it's just that morality has dried up, like holy water in a stoup. Everything changes.

We used to figure things in inches, feet and yards. You could picture it, even if you were lousy at figuring. A guy six feet tall is more impressive than a hulk who's only one metre eighty. You just had to be able to count. Back then, you could measure land just by walking it, foot by foot. For multiples of feet, we had yards and even rods or poles. And we estimated wood in cords, which had nothing to do with the pants we were wearing.

Still, I wouldn't really want to turn the clock back. We had to modernize so we rethought America in metric and then had to change all the scales from pounds to kilos and recalibrate all the gas pumps from gallons to litres. It even got political, with the Anglos convinced it was a revolution cooked up by the Québécois on account of Napoleon and all that. As if we were going to get back at them for the Queen of England by shoving a French system down their throats, centimetre by centimetre, sending their imperial measures the way of the dodo. Everything passes.

With time, the new system took over in industry from Atlantic to Pacific. When it comes to real life though, maybe Canada's less modern. In a country where the weather gets people down it's not easy to take the plunge all at once, sink or swim. Your nose tells you pretty fast when the temperature gets below zero in metric, as long as you're not an Eskimo. It's logical I know, zero's when water freezes, but when you're living at thirty degrees below, that kind of logic leaves you cold.

The first winters in metric were merciless. I'd learned in Fahrenheit and if I was warm it was in Fahrenheit I felt it. Our government kept telling us the United States would have to follow our lead. What a bum steer that was! The Americans just stayed the way they were before. So I began listening to American radio, out of Vermont, to hear if the weather was going to be frigid or the opposite. They never missed a beat in the U.S. weather reports, just kept on playing the same old tune. They'll take the cake every time, those Americans, right to the last crumb.

It was the Americans who Monsieur Rosen got the idea of a security agency from, he told me. It happened on a trip to New York. In a Rotary Club speech at the World Trade Centre, he heard that crime and fear of crime were bound to keep on growing. New York was a leader in urban violence even then; you could see it sprayed in living colour on walls and subway cars. Monsieur Rosen was thinking of his customers and yardgoods stores, of course. And I must say he does sell us his uniforms pretty cheap.

In New York twenty years ago there were companies hiring out armed drivers, the middle class shut themselves up in buildings with security guards at the door, and the too-rich were always afraid their offspring were going to get kidnapped. So fear of being robbed blind was the mother of invention.

2. By habit, I number everything I write. It's an addiction I got hooked on at the Baie d'Urfé Public Library, where Employment Canada had found me a little job putting

children's books back on the shelves. I'd made a pretty nice little job of it, too, because I couldn't resist the books and kept losing myself in the texts and illustrations. I discovered *Gulliver's Travels* in my thirties! The boss lady gave me the sack though she was nice about it, said I did too much reading to work in a library. Still, I left knowing a bit about the codes, so I was that much ahead.

These days I write things down and number them so as not to forget. I mean to say, if Maman's losing her memory bit by bit, the same thing's going to happen to me for sure. It's genetic, I read that in the paper last Sunday. Already I find certain words getting lost and however hard I root around I can't get them back. Then there are names that disappear too. What *was* the barman's name at the Hotel Canada?

Each time I leave the John H. Drinkwater Institute in Boston, where Maman is drifting away bit by bit, I think of those people who learn La Fontaine fables by heart to keep their brain cells working. A lot further ahead they'll be when they've forgotten everything but "The Grasshopper and The Ant." If *my* neurons go soft, at least I'll be able to reread what I've written. That's what I tell myself when I see my mother's face wrinkle up in despair because she knows she's forgetting, the way you know it when you're going crazy.

3. Monsieur Rosen claims a security guard pays for his keep five times over by what he prevents in vandalism and shoplifting. The classified ad in the *Journal de Montréal* said, "Your presence will be invaluable." It really went to my heart.

I'm sensitive, I need to be needed. Besides, I was looking for work at that point. There aren't that many jobs out there when you haven't got as far as university. Even if you have. In the last ten years I've seen requirements go sky high across the board. You've got to speak three languages just to answer the telephone. Soon you'll have to show them a degree in urban studies before they'll take you on as a garbage collector.

When you're in kindergarten you're encouraged to be creative, your drawings get pinned up on the wall and taped on the frig door and even on the way up the stairs, but later, in real life, there isn't room for fantasy any more. So I've decided to stow my creativity deep in my pocket, put my handkerchief on top of it, then my keys, then my fist.

I mean, it wasn't easy to conform at first, to knuckle under. Play the poodle in a tutu in their megabucks circus, a teetotum with a smile in their multi-floored emporium. In the end, after some knocks on the noggin and boots in the butt, I finally got the idea. I wasn't a total moron. I told myself the uniform would get me by without argument. I was fed to the teeth with being chewed out—"So you want to be different, Monsieur Galarneau?" So I went from being singular to being plural. Clamped the lid on the pot so they wouldn't hear me boil. I said to myself, "Galarneau, you're going to toe the line, you're not a child, you're going to keep your cool; humanity is counting on you; you have to shoulder your responsibilities."

I'd showed up at the company office one rainy Saturday morning. The secretary I spoke to was as grouchy as the weather but I didn't react. I filled in the forms, gave my references, wrote in my last three jobs and declared I was single, which was true in fact if not in law.

Monsieur Rosen looked at me hard over his half-moon glasses and his nose was inquisitorial. "Are you in favour of law and order?" he asked me severely.

"If I were frank with you," I replied cheerfully," I'd say I was rather more anarchist, but since it's a disorderly world we live in, being a security guard is closer to my ideal than any other job, I'm sure of it."

"An anarchist? My grandfather in Kraków was an anarchist. He ended up in prison."

"Well, I imagine he wore a uniform in prison, didn't he? That's it! I want to be like your grandfather!"

Monsieur Rosen raised his bushy eyebrows. He raised them so high I thought they were going to take off like butterflies. I'd disarmed him, the big boss all tight-assed over his principles, eminent leader of men, by-the-yard millionaire and verily general of an army of parasites feeding on fear.

He turned to a paunchy old fellow standing behind him who seemed more grandfather than flunky. "What d'you think, Jean-Charles?" he said. "This young fellow's pretty quick and smooth with the answers, but will he be able to handle the teenagers?" Then he turned back to me and added, "Jean-Charles is my right hand, he's been with Harry Sécurité since the beginning."

Jean-Charles wasn't really keen on giving an opinion because he'd known since way back that Monsieur Rosen made his own decisions. So he just mumbled something with an echo in his tubes that must have been from emphysema, as he seemed to be doing all the time.

"I'm going to try you out," Monsieur Rosen told me. "You're going to have to watch some clever women, specially the ones that come in clutches from New Delhi or Port-au-Prince. They chatter all round you till they make your head swim, then before you know it they've got a roll of twenty-dollar-a-yard pillow-lace in the bag, right under your nose. You'd better keep your eyes peeled!"

"That should be twenty dollars a metre ..." I told him, but we were speaking French so what I said was "*vingt dollars le mètre*".

"*C'est moi le maître!*" Monsieur Rosen shot back. He *was* the boss, of course. Then he laughed with a hissing noise as if he was giving off steam, proud of the French pun he had just made. This was the Harry who had learned Yiddish on his uncle's knee and English on St. Urbain Street. Then French on the job from Jean-Charles, after the law changed the relationships between principals and subordinates.

"For the first few weeks you can wear an old uniform I've got. If you fill the bill, I'll sell you two and dock your pay twenty dollars a week for eight weeks, custom tailoring thrown in. As far as the rest goes, at Harry Sécurité we have good labour relations, no union, a day off a week."

"I don't really need a day off," I protested, "what I want is a job. I want to make myself useful."

"We're going to get along, I can sense that," Monsieur Rosen replied. And so we did from that day on. The next morning I went with Jean-Charles to learn how to be an agent of order and security in today's society. Have to do what we have to do.

4. One, two, buckle my shoe. Three, four, shut the door. If it weren't for counting rhymes, would I still remember the sound of water lapping on the shore of Lake St. Louis?

To spark Maman's interest, I begin reciting this one for her over the phone and she chimes in. That's what memory is:

15

a familiar old drawer.

I make the rounds of the second-hand dealers, buying all the old record albums, sheet music, song books, comb through the fleamarkets, it's the old tunes I have to have, they're the only ones she'll sing along with me. Doris Day for the twilight of Maman's life. Maurice Chevalier—in English! Each time I hang up the phone, tired and hoarse, I wonder who'll be there to sing for me. Who will recite me lines by Dylan, Brassens, Charlebois, Lennon, Rivard?

Seventy-eight, forty-five, thirty-three little revolutions a minute and we're off.

It was my idea to put Maman in a home in Boston and my brothers agreed. So many years had already passed since she'd escaped to Lowell, Massachusetts to be with her old-maid cousins. In fact, a hundred years ago when nobody had enough to eat, half her family joined the Great Migration south to the textile mills of New England.

Anyway, the John H. Drinkwater Institute is run by Jean Boileau who still understands Maman's language and mine, even though he's changed his name. He gave us a deal that took account of the distance so we could get down to see her once in a while. Good old Boileau! He's invented a tequila-based cocktail that he'd like to see bear his name. Three Boileaus and away you go! Maman took a fancy to them—why hide it?

5. Jean-Charles put me wise from the start. The key to the job, he said, was to look like a soldier when there were

crowds around and get one's nose in a book when things were slack.

"It doesn't matter if you're assigned to a supermarket or offices or a high school or the ticket booth of an underground parking lot, reading's the real secret," he told me. "In some situations you can watch TV, but that has disastrous effects. The screen sucks up your neurons and your senses go dead, so as a night watchman you get to be as much use as a burned-out battery."

Jean-Charles is like a non-smoker, he's convinced it's his duty to help humanity make wholesome choices. He's a man of his generation, I mean, he was born before the Second World War, in the midst of the Depression, which didn't make for optimists. He's taught me some tricks though, like how to use mirrors without letting on, and how to look faraway, as if you're woolgathering. Whatever you do, when you're patrolling in a small space you mustn't move around too much, it puts the pigeons on edge. You have to know the birds you're after.

My first days at Monsieur Harry's were easy to take. Young girls, come to look at crêpes and laces for their wedding dresses, would brush by me discreetly, watched by dumpy, hawk-eyed ogress mothers with mustaches. The mothers and daughters would parade up and down the main aisle. In the two models, destiny was plain to see: the same chins, the same nose lines; one with porcelain-smooth face, the other wrinkled and gravel-voiced. Inevitably; it's just a matter of time.

The one enemy on earth I'm really afraid of is time. I would have liked a glacial volcano to erupt there and then and bury us, freeze us all in a crystal-clear block of ice so these faces would be preserved for eternity just the way they were. This was pretty dumb as ideas go. The most beautiful girl in the world, held motionless like a insect preserved in acrylic, would have no reason to be. Life means putting up with wrinkles.

In the back room of his store, above the accountant's desk, Monsieur Rosen kept a hodgepodge of books. The first one I put my hand on was a philosophical treatise. In English. It was kind of heavy going but I cottoned onto it and read it in a few days, propped against bolts of silk. All I've retained of it is one idea, but such a powerful idea it dazzles me even now. I might describe it this way: what some call a soul and others the life principle or breath of God (each religion has its own term and it hardly matters which), this strange mechanism that beats the measure for our breathing is *time*. It appears at the precise instant a weary sperm penetrates a fertile ovum. The metre thereupon begins ticking in the taxi of life. Not everybody rides the same route, but that's not the crux of it. I mean, time is not there to be taken, it exists *in itself.*

I am time, time is in my own hands, but I can neither watch it go by nor be rid of it, it's a tick, a solitary worm, a cancer. Einstein, in his belief that time is slowed by interstellar space travel, was utterly, completely wrong; it's the cosmonaut who slacks off. In my work, an idea like this makes you think, if I might say, in real time. In a factory at night, with rounds to make every two hours, twenty doors to check, seventeen clocks to punch, you walk and you punch those clocks and you've just seen seven minutes of your life flit away. In fact, you're the one who can really measure time because you're the one who goes by, unseen by the world. A fine idea, this. Killing time means killing yourself. But in order to know who and where you are, you have to be ready to waste time and even give it.

There was one thing about being a security man I liked from the beginning. Harry Sécurité officers don't carry arms, they work with their bodies and eyes. "Body language," as Jean-Charles said, using Monsieur Rosen's expression. It's true, in order to stop a rumpus sometimes all you have to do is slowly, deliberately cross your arms. This was not one of those agencies that specialize in thick-headedness, mugs with glazed eyes, Cro-Magnon jaws and brandy noses. We've all got our own personal techniques but it's the results that count, no two ways about it. So on the fourth day Jean-Charles gave me a whole store to guard, solo, in Rosemount. In the middle of September! When mothers are flocking to clothe their brats! I stood the test, spoke with all my muscles, and read two gangster novels for my own education. You never know.

I filled the bill all right and Monsieur Rosen sent me to his tailor's. I now have six uniforms hanging in the closet at home, four of which are out of fashion. We've lived together, those uniforms and I, so I daren't throw them out or give them away.

There was Véronique too but she's not in the closet any more because she's gone to Vancouver. Nowadays it's the girls who go and the man who gets left at home. I don't know what gives them such itchy feet. They smoke. They work. They cruise. Then they move in with you and get their clothes in your closet, but their suitcases are never far away. Véronique walked out with her earphones on, telling me she was supposed to go round the world before she was thirty. She's going to have to hurry up! She's got one thing going for her though: her astrologer, who leads her by the nose, works in a travel agency.

We shared the closet for nearly three years. I can still smell her perfume in it. We'd caught each other's scent one stormy summer night when both of us were stuck under Loew's marquee, wet and shivering, after seeing *Sophie's Choice*, each of us alone. In all that rain there was only one taxi to be had and we shared it. Her dress clung to her body, I don't know why she made me think of a beaver with its head up and its fur wet. She invited me in to dry off and talk about the movie. Her hair began to curl with the heat but mine stayed stiff as a poker. She put a Leonard Cohen tape on her hi-fi, etcetera, etcetera.

She wasn't expecting Travolta, but still, I think she found me rather predictable. She loved insecurity, caves, danger, so she would have liked me to be a speleologist. I told her that an agent of Monsieur Rosen's was a constant mark for murderers. She wasn't particularly excited to hear it. She moved in because she'd had enough of getting half dressed and then having to go home to change her shoes after spending the night with me. It had been easier for me; like a scout, always prepared, one uniform at her apartment and one at Fabre Street.

Véronique was well known, she was the one who presented the winning lottery balls on television. I'd drawn a winning number for sure. We were meant for each other. Had all the same likes and dislikes. In everything. Books, dawdling round the streets. Opera, which both of us hated. In three years there was only one thing we disagreed about. Her numerologist had told her she should be the mother of the first baby of the year 2000. I was willing, but that meant it had to be conceived between three and four in the morning in the first week of April 1999. At that hour I'm at work. I offered to donate sperm for freezing so all she'd have to do was go to the bank at the appropriate time. Trouble was, she wanted a baby conceived *with* love. We had conflicting schedules. I'm head guard at the Garland Mall, a contract Monsieur Rosen landed not so long ago. Seven guards during the day and two after closing, on rotation. Sometimes I keep the night shift for myself, asking for the moon you might say. There are so many

20

books to read since Véronique's been gone!

Anyway, I'm a night owl, like Maman when she was younger. We've got vampire blood in our veins. My two brothers are the same. Jacques is an insomniac, keeps convenience-store hours. Arthur never sleeps but since he left for San Francisco I really don't know any more, maybe he sleeps with his eyes open like a crocodile. It was a close-knit family we had, the three of us, then one day it came apart like a can that's been on the shelf too long. A can of worms with cares to spare. The people you love don't live forever. A day comes when they've used up the time they've been living. Then life implodes.

I think my brothers were a bit hurt when I filled up my notebooks and got to writing about us that first time. When it comes down to it, the only people who should write are the Jules Vernes. I mean, works of pure imagination don't hurt anyone. But it's all so unimportant, really. There's too much fuss made over writers. And writers make too much fuss over their books. We should get some perspective on it all. Monsieur Rosen told me he had a childhood friend who's become a famous writer in the United States and who runs down the Jews in all his novels. "I think he's got a point," he said. "If I want to listen to pleasant, predictable things, I go to a synagogue."

Harry Rosen's a free man who doesn't believe in God or the devil either. He believes in business. Making money. These days as we approach the end of a century that will not see a child of mine born, the only thing that makes sense is business, along with its new cathedrals.

6. The Garland Mall has two floors and a lower-street level. It's not the biggest shopping mall in town but it's one of the nicest. A hundred and twenty stores, two department-store branches, eighteen ethnic restaurants, all clustered around a public square. At noon when all the tables are occupied there's bustle and chatter and a warm, friendly smell of humanity.

Monsieur Rosen obtained this contract for Harry Sécurité because his agents look good. We complement the décor of the place.

Nothing is left to chance in a shopping mall these days. Specialists by the dozen have plotted the crowd traffic patterns, worked out what fragrances should be released and at which hours of the day. Cooking smells, for instance, ought not to encroach on the evergreen scents wafting about the menswear displays. As important as attention to the sense of smell is the choice of colours, which are soft, maternal and reassuring in open spaces and stimulating in the approaches to the stores. All must encourage the eye to find the merchandise enticing. Incredible care has been lavished on the lighting and alternating areas of light and shadow aid our surveillance of passing shoppers. Fundamental guidelines (never locate a high-fashion boutique beside a food store) and behavioural studies, if judiciously applied, ensure the success of this kind of enterprise. A shopping mall is like a psychological treatise in three dimensions. We security guards, Jean-Charles says, are the fourth dimension. He means that we should be invisible but in charge.

7. Jean-Charles has gone from being Monsieur Rosen's right-hand man to being his chauffeur. He may have a hard time getting behind the wheel because his legs are kind of short, but he gets to keep the car after hours, which suits us fine. When he has nothing to do or while the boss is at a meeting, Jean-Charles does the rounds of the second-hand and bargain bookstores. He fills up the trunk of the Pontiac with all kinds of books he's bought. The boss's car is our bookmobile.

When I read a great book (like *One Hundred Years of Solitude*, which I devoured voraciously during my quiet nights), I try to imagine the last person who held it. To me, the more stained the cover, the more dog-eared the pages, the more valuable a book should be. Other eyes have read these same lines. Where did they linger? It seems to me that each line, when other readers have lent their personal voices to it, grows in depth and humanity. And those biographies and other non-fictions with yellow highlighting and marginal notes—Lord, they're beautiful!

A book I've got inside is like an apartment I'm living in. If it's a second-hand book, I'm interested in the previous tenant. Sometimes a reader has affixed an ex-libris or signed and dated the fly-leaf. Then I take the phone book and try to trace the person. It's endless and you have to go about it right. First the homonyms in the phone book. "Good-day, Madam, excuse me for disturbing you, but have you read *Les Évadés de la nuit* by André Langevin?" Most of the time they hang up on me. Some people want to know why. I explain. "I've found a book with your name in it, yes, Berthiaume. No, no, not Céline, it's a T., for Thérèse, could it be? Or Tancrède perhaps? Oh, what a pity! You wouldn't know a T. Berthiaume, would you?"

Around seven o'clock one evening I came across a reader

who touched my heart. Her name was written in big round letters in a book of Chagall reproductions—he's the painter of love and marriage. I was a little cross because no one should sell off a book of Chagall reproductions. He was such a soft-hearted painter that he lived till he was nearly a hundred. All his paintings tell love stories; he had a talent for making landscapes resonate and skies rejoice. Chagall characters are as free as the air that they often float in among fairground balloons. It passed my understanding how anyone would exchange such a book for anything in the world. I said as much, testily, befitting the way I felt, after verifying that I had the right person at the other end of the line. Her name was Antoinette Lachapelle and she was eighty-two years old. She had ceded the book to a St. Catherine Street bookseller in order to buy a morsel of bread. Chagall would have understood and I'm not a total nitwit, but with my sainted temper I'd thoughtlessly fallen on an indigent little old lady. Politely, I begged permission to return her picture book. The next day I arrived bearing gifts of flowers and fruit, but she'd up and left during the night. As ethereal as a Chagall bride!

It's a silly game, I know, but when I'm sitting there in front of the surveillance system's ten monitors, which often look down on nothing at all, I like this kind of hunt that allows me to keep watching while telephoning. The most critical monitors are the ones in the underground parking garage. Section 4B, Zebra. Giraffe Section is less problematical. It isn't that the garage is a zoo; to help customers not to lose their cars, which they often do, the crowd traffic engineers have devised signs featuring African animals like lions and hippopotami which, stencilled on columns, remind people which waterhole is theirs. It's a useful location system. We've even had our very own murder under the sign of the elephants. Drug dealers imagining they were in the jungle, no doubt. The victim's car stayed there two days with its door open, cordoned off with ribbons by the police. A BMW like the one Marise would have loved to have.

I was twenty then and wanted to be a successful business-man. Marise would have settled for being rich. My book came between us though. When I began to write in quiet moments, specially in the afternoons, she imagined herself becoming famous overnight. She wanted to be the heroine of the story. I was the wrong writer for her. She was a pretty brunette with nice round breasts; my brother couldn't say no. She threw me over for him because he was a television scriptwriter; a question of antennae. I couldn't blame her, I had my notebooks to fill. Exit Marise. Last year I saw her queuing up for a movie; she'd dyed her hair blonde and her breasts were sort of like melons. "Don't you recognize me?" she said. I just glared at her. I'm pretty impressive in my uniform. I hope she was sorry then. I act tough as if I don't care, but Marise was my first great love. My first heartbreak too, after Papa's death.

Since Antoinette Lachapelle, I haven't been phoning peo-ple the same way. I put questions to myself. Who would probably have read Ramuz? I picture the person before mak-ing my approach. I wouldn't want to go stirring up any more heartache. You never can tell with second-hand books. What has most likely put them on the market? A divorce, a death, a separation? It's easier to negotiate custody of a child than divide up a library built by two people together. She bought *La Condition humaine* but he was the one who read it. Who should have custody of the books? Which of the two will they grow with best? Some picnic! So the couple settles it by sell-ing off the lot for a few pennies. I've heard about it; they tell me their life stories on the phone. I'm a good listener. And when I get back to the books, I read them differently.

8. So as not to go to sleep on the highway I used to recite everything I knew by heart aloud, even Our Father and Ave Maria. I was driving a semi-trailer from Drummondville to the United States, peatmoss in one direction and rolls of barbed wire in the other. Before I got to be a Harry Sécurité guard I was free-trade personified. A Trucker. Enriching it damn well wasn't! I mean, sometimes a trip would swallow up a whole week of my life. For time off I got forty-eight hours in the city of my choice. Ham 'n' eggs, toast, coffee, round and round and round he goes and where he'll land nobody knows. Maybe in Never-Never Land. You had to hear it to believe the Americans calling me "Glarno" or "Gerlno". I couldn't put them right. I wasn't going to say, "Boys, I bear the name of the sun itself, so I'll thank you to address me correctly." The Americans only know one language and that's basic English; they've even taught it to their computers.

I'd stopped writing at this time. Necessarily—when you're driving a trailer train you have to keep your hands on the wheel. But with no one to talk to I had plenty of time for thinking. I used to think at seventy miles an hour, a wee bit faster than the speed limit. The radio at max, Johnny Cash or his kind, beautiful weeping guitars filling the cab. What went through my head was like some of the texts I'm rereading now, what the Americans call "stream of thoughts", I think.

I was driving for Bordeleau Transport, the bulk specialists. I'll admit now I did so much driving in the U.S. and was so impressed with the power, wealth and vitality of American cities that I made an official application to the U.S. Immigration Office in Washington, D.C. It's nothing to be ashamed of. Our ancestors explored these areas before any of the rest did. I saw French names all over, from the Carolinas to Louisiana. My idea was simple: I wanted to disappear, have no more ties with anyone. My brothers could get by without me. Maman was already in the States. I remembered her saying, often when I seemed to be daydreaming, "A penny for your thoughts, François." I had penny-ante dreams, it's true— I wanted to take French leave, change seasons. Deep down, what I wanted was to forget the Quebec Carnival and go and wallow under the palm trees. Atlanta. Jacksonville. Chattanooga. Nobody knew me there and I could start over without the burden of being a Galarneau. Buy my own truck.

It turned out to be a million-dollar dream. There had to be references, the consulate in Montreal wanted twenty different documents, and I let it drop. I still get to read quite a lot in American though. What surprises me most in novels of the South (I mean, compared to Natashquan or Montreal, everything on the map's pretty well south) is how often the hero of the story is a writer. In Anatole France country that's less frequent. And then these writer-heroes drink gigantic quantities of scotch and bourbon. Maybe it depends what a writer can afford.

9. Being happy is relatively simple, really. I probably took too long to figure this out. What you need is stability and plush surroundings. Thanks to Harry Sécurité, my stability's guaranteed—a forty-eight hour week—and with the surroundings I have at Garland, I'm in caviar. The store windows overflow with luxurious woollen suits and sequined evening dresses, hundreds of magnificent leather shoes are displayed on

velvet cushions, pyramids of copper cookware glisten next to towers of hand-painted china, and in some displays there's as much fur as you'd see in a zoo. All the products of skilled hands are there: furniture, bedding, toys, food, clocks and watches, electronics, confectionery; a panorama to gratify an infinity of hearts' desires. I can feel fulfilled without needing to possess a single object. It's Christmas and Easter all year round. Each festal occasion is succeeded by another: Father's Day, Mother's Day, St. Patrick's Day, Valentine's Day, the bedlinen festival; gay festoons of paper streamers surround me on every side.

At night, when only security lighting garbs the corridors, I walk the path of occidental, Christian civilization with keys in hand. In the half-light, the abundance wakens the same feeling of supernatural presence that used to fill our hearts in church when we were children. The trouble is, it sometimes also makes my stomach heave; too much caviar at Garland, not enough bread and water in the Sahel. I stop at the Travel Boutique and look for some unsuspected destination. More often than not, I end up with my head over a toilet bowl.

10. I don't know if it was Rasputin or some other court holy man who set my brother Arthur on the contestation route, but he was certainly bitten by someone. And once Arthur is under way, you might as well try stopping a locomotive with your bare hands. He slept with Frantz Fanon, quoted Marx and always had Marcuse in the left-hand pocket of his red jacket. Mao, Mau-Mau, Castro. I remember the

first demo he took me to, outside Place des Arts in the heart of Montreal. We'd hitchhiked all the way from Île Perrot, telling our benefactors, car after car, what benefits the revolution would bring them.

The point of that demonstration was rather vague; it consisted of booing bourgeois Montréalers on their way to a concert. We were part of a group of newly bearded youths who had absolutely no desire to sit quietly in rows facing a symphony orchestra anyway. All music lovers are bourgeois, the monkey suits the musicians wear prove it. The police were on their great horses, not all of which were exactly gentle. The hoof of one of the quadrupeds grazed Arthur's boot and the pain Arthur suffered that night confirmed him a true revolutionary. To tell the truth I would have liked to hear the music, but all I was allowed to hear were catcalls. When the sun disappeared and the temperature dropped, the demonstrators lit a big bonfire of their placards and sticks. They sang anthems and shouted slogans which were as quickly blown away by the wind as the sparks from the fire.

I went home. I was kind of depressed; I had my hot-dog stand, my notebooks, I was a cook by trade. Arthur stayed at the front. I wasn't running away, I just felt out of place there. If I can explain, let's say I like people but when they're in bunches I can do without them. I don't know "the people" *personally*, I mean, they're anonymous, go around in crowds, grumble, suffer, and look for light from luminaries like Arthur, my brother. I'll stick with my old flashlight, my Eveready; to each his own torch. And when it comes to flashlights, it's always been more my style to take one under the covers to read Ray Bradbury by than to go round waving it. If the earth gets to be unlivable we'll just have to leave it behind and go to another planet. Then when it comes time to gather on the day of the Great Departure, Harry Sécurité's topflight team will be just the one to guide the earthlings to the white airships waiting on the ramp assigned for interstellar flight.

11. Arthur had always been, shall I say, the most aerial of the three of us. He was the one who used to climb to the highest branches of the tree we had built the Vampires' Retreat in. He was always hard to pin down. As a fledgling accountant, he ran charity campaigns for the clergy. He was good at choosing the themes and best times of the year and he organized door-to-door canvassing, using the necessary pressure. He paid himself a healthy percentage and lived at celestial altitudes in a downtown penthouse. The pyramid collapsed when the income tax inspectors decided to get their noses into his books. If he didn't go to prison, it must be said, it was because the archbishopric got him off for fear of scandal.

I don't know the details of his downfall because at the time I was in an institution, a large hospital on the Rivière des Prairies. I'd wound my spring a bit too tight and everything had jammed; I couldn't even cry any more. It was hoped that here I'd get my feet back on the ground. My room was bathed in a soft light that reached my bed through the russet leaves of tall poplars. All I had to do was eat, read and sleep; the institution was banking on the peacefulness and beauty of the site to straighten me out.

It was Jacques who brought me to this bucolic spot run by an old college classmate. The shrink at this paradise was a strapping, frizzy-haired fellow who was a lot crazier than I was, which is perhaps why he was there all year round. I saw him twice a week when he gave me a battery of tests and pressed me to talk about my early childhood.

"Guilt precedes the act, dear boy, Freud proved it beyond a doubt." Doctor Staedtler had not known Freud in person of course, he was a disciple; there's nothing worse. Without disciples Jesus himself would have been forgotten and so would the bearded Viennese. If you're going to be famous you have to stick to being vague and pick up some disciples, which is something I should have done. Ah, Oedipus! That absent Father. It was for Him Christ got himself crucified. When we came around to Maman, the doctor wanted me to associate chocolate and caca. I was a classic case, he told me. Papa's death when I was very young had traumatized me, I kept hearing his voice in my subconscious. Like Joan of Arc?

The first signs of schizoid behaviour begin somewhere around the age of twenty, according to the white-jackets. It was their job to look into this idea of mine that somebody had implanted electrodes in my head so as to control me. I was right too! What is all that twaddle by analysts, specialists and television announcers if not the planting of so many little needles in our brains in order to make us turn one way or another? I had disconnected from all this through my own writing, describing things the better to circumscribe the perfidy all around me. Since then I've read and studied a lot, even if I don't have any diplomas to prove it. I'm an autodidact, which is faster than hoofing it.

12. I finished writing *Salut Galarneau!* at the institution. It ended up being a novel because I wanted to reshape the events, skew the characters, invent anecdotes in order to make all of it more true and less real. It's pretty faithful as far as the details go, I mean the details about my business activities and the best grilled hot dogs in town. I was ahead of my time. Twenty years later, "entrepreneurship" was all anyone was talking about. Entrepreneur*shit*! No man is a prophet ...

The book brought me a lot of mail, which Dr. Staedtler read aloud to me. I say aloud to be polite; I think a patient must have bitten him in the balls, which had raised his voice a few octaves. Most readers wanted to tell me that in their families too, in the Gaspé, on Lac Saint-Jean, in Saint-Chrysostome or Sainte-Rose-du-Dégelis, as in my family, the sun was called Galarneau; it made me happy to discover I had so many cousins. Other readers suggested explanations. Some thought Galarneau came from an Amerindian name, something like *Gawano* which was the word for daybreak in Huron or Iroquois. Others said it proved I was still a dumb little shit hung up on distilled Walt Disney anthropomorphism: Bambi and Galarneau fighting one and the same battle. The most interesting explanation came from a native of Britanny who talked about the *vent de galerne*, the west-north-west wind, the one that cleans the sky, sweeping out the clouds and bringing back the sun.

The Galarneau brothers, even born to another family with an engineer father and a golf-champion mother and living in a Hong Kong suburb, would not have traced a different course. The die is cast at birth, that's known; from the moment of delivery everything is predictable. Maman doesn't even remember the first sounds I made or whether I was born on a rainy Thursday or a sunny Sunday, but destiny was in attendance. Goddamn destiny! The only thing that can throw it off track, I know now, is the right book at the right moment, and then the celestial fortune-teller can go fly a kite!

When I shut myself up to write in the last few weeks before going to the institution, I lost a lot of weight. The white-jackets got me back in shape with shepherd's pie. I think it's called "shepherd's" because of the fluffy white mashed potatoes on top. I didn't used to serve it at my stand and I was wrong; if I'd had shepherd's pie on the menu I'd still be king.

Staedtler gave me the run of his personal library, half scientific books and the other half detective stories by the ton, stacked all over the place, higgledy-piggledy enough to muddle any plot. Below Jung's *Modern Myth*, gun-totin' American dreams. I began to read the lot, and roamed the streets of Chicago, Los Angeles, San Francisco and Philadelphia in the company of private eyes. Now I didn't want to leave the hospital. This was proof that my mental health was restored: "A true psychotic does not willingly remain confined," they say. They don't know what they're talking about. Between the covers of a book, one is never confined.

13. Jacques came to take me home from the hospital. Things were already less rosy between him and Marise, who was doing more than her share of crabbing. I was kind of glad.

Jacques said, "I can't talk and write at the same time just to please her!"

I thought, Your turn, brother! I said, "She needs attention."

"Me too, but not all the time!" Jacques fumed.

"Are you trying to tell me you sleep with her so I won't have to?"

I wasn't holding it against him. You can't order up love like a case of 24 from the corner store. But just the name Marise made my chest hurt so much that not crying like a man was something I almost wasn't able to do.

Jacques had brought me to a sunny terrace where we killed off several big, cold bottles under a yellow umbrella. He talked to me about the success of my book. He was pretty proud of himself for finding me a publisher. I was already somewhere else.

"What are you figuring on doing? You're going to carry on?" He meant, Are you going to write some more, get published, make a career of it, sign books, get on radio, take my place?

"Don't worry, Jacques, it was therapy. You're the writer in the family."

The beer was good in those big, caressable plastic glasses, they were soft and sweet, like breasts in my hands. I suckled a bucketful from them. A Fifty, an O'Keefe, a Laurentide, a Blue, a Bud. Sitting in the sun.

"You see, François, you were writing off the top of your head but for me it isn't therapy, so I have to find the time."

"You will, Jacques."

"One day I'll get into it."

"Get into the beer!"

"The time to write, that's what I'm missing. Marise doesn't understand."

I should have told him, The time is in you, Jacques, but I hadn't yet discovered Monsieur Rosen's philospher on the shelf in back of his store. This is proof once again that meeting up with the right author at the right moment can change your life. Yes, change your life.

14. In the months that followed, Jacques insisted I get out and around for the sake of my mental health. Arthur too, dragging me from one demonstration to the next. A mania with him. Since his galling experience at Place des Arts, like Claudel who suddenly found grace in Notre Dame Cathedral, he had only one aim and that was to agitate. He was a professional provocateur. Finished and done with were charities, raffles, streetcorner thermometers. When golden agers marched on the premier's office or women organized a nighttime parade to overcome fear, Arthur and his little pals managed to stir up the neighbourhood, attract thugs and thieves, bait the forces of law and order. The minute he appeared in a crowd, it was magnetic; bottles broke on the pavement, stones whistled through the air, windows shattered. I cut out at that point, telling him, "There are other ways to get on TV. We've got a brother in the business."

The next summer Arthur went into retreat with the Trappists. The Cistercian monastery was out of town and the monks offered him silence, a garden to hoe, ripening cheese to be tended at dawn, and meditation sessions that today's gurus purvey for exorbitant sums. I went to visit him. Those men on retreat were living pretty well in fact because the Trappists were doing the cooking. The monastery reminded me of the hospital I'd been in: the same mortared stone walls, the same white-painted windows, the same poplar trees. Although

Arthur's mentors wore sackcloth, they were perhaps as crazy as mine. I envied him for the monastery library, the leather-bound books smelled so good. A book with gilt-edged pages changes the way you look at things.

But this wasn't Arthur's calling. A few weeks later he had a job as a teacher on the small Maria reservation on the Baie des Chaleurs. It was a rainy summer in Montreal that year and the greenhouse effect was giving the summer vegetation a strong, heady smell. The maple trees that occupied the sky above the rooftops invaded the streets with their shaggy branches. Mount Royal looked like a window box between two clouds. So when Arthur arrived to begin his new job he was surprised to find how dry the air was in the Gaspé that same summer, how abundant the light and immense the sky.

15. Maria, September 17, 1969

Dear François, I've never been a good photographer and here the sea reflects our Galarneau a giorno! In these parts it's impossible to take a good picture, the shadows are so deep and all else is washed out by the light. I'm sending you these anyway so you can use your imagination, that's up your alley. The first is a picture of the brilliant mathematics teacher. Since I'm teaching Micmac children, what you see me holding are pebbles, and you can picture a whole basket of them at my feet. The pebble method is imperative with unruly kids. But there's a practical angle too—the stones are agates and when we've finished adding, multiplying and subtracting them, we polish them! As you can see I haven't changed, except for the beard which you'll think is pretty thick. I'm not a Cistercian any more. I've decided to play White Father. Those are missionary whiskers I'm sporting; the revolutionary fuzz dropped out one hair at a time.

The second picture—as hazy as the book Jacques keeps yakking about—shows a cabin in Canada, in a vague kind of way, somewhere in the woods at Maria. Look carefully. That's tarpaper covering the planks. Behind are a few birches marking the edge of a small wood. And the last picture, little brother, is one of my class. You thought you recognized huggable little tots? They're imps of eight to twelve and all they do is play in the long grass all day. I have the laborious task of teaching them to think. I'm not sure it's a very sound idea. What do you think? Will you write me soon?

I've kept all Arthur's letters because at that time the Montreal World's Fair was just over and I had the idea of getting to be Jacques's documentalist. I mean, I'd collect documents like newspaper clippings and quickly jotted notes and Jacques would use them to write television programs. Jacques wasn't against the plan but that's not the way things are done at Radio-Canada. They've got professional researchers for professional writers and collective agreements and union meetings, and I was just too amateur. Anyway, today I'm glad I kept the pictures and all. Specially since Arthur dropped out of sight a while after.

The habitual language on Indian reservations is Creole Shakespearean, which is also the language of the federal government and other tiresome things. So Arthur set himself to learn Micmac and did it so well that in eight months the bearded little teacher was in charge of the tribe's books. He kept the cooperative's accounts and managed the wigwam-shaped two-storey store that sold Indianware. For years the Micmacs had been selling little woven baskets, bows, necklaces and snowshoes strung with rawhide to passing tourists.

In the village chief's house, Arthur found a copy of *Nadja* by André Breton with an inscription in the author's own hand, dated 1942. The European had swapped the book for a pair of snowshoes belonging to the chief's uncle, the chief recalled. People would have trouble imagining even the high priest of surrealism in Montparnasse after the war, waddling on snowshoes across the road between the *clous* with a *ceinture fléchée* round his waist and a clay pipe in his teeth, then ordering a *petit blanc* at the bar and drinking a toast to the tribe at Maria. That's because they're short on imagination, they're too prosaic.

My brother Arthur wasn't short on imagination. He taught the women to polish agates and mount them in silver; he knew a thing or two about clawing. The Micmacs opened a jewelry counter, the jewelry wasn't exactly teepee typical but the money rolled in and the chief was happy. A year later Arthur became Nadja Astac, alias The Lobster, an adopted son of Maria. He was reddened by the sun where his long Oblate beard didn't shield him, and he ate, drank and bickered with the elders every evening.

I can't say that Breton's book has profoundly influenced the local mores, my dear François. The pages of Nadja *were't even cut. Still, I think the surrealist spirit was already embedded in the Micmac way of life. Did you know that a hammer has a thousand uses here? It can even hang from a clothes-line to steady it against the wind off the sea. In winter most of the television sets lie dormant on verandas. Is there an iron in the refrigerator? The Micmacs don't press their pants. The Micmacs are never pressed.*

16. Nadja Astac alias Arthur Galarneau might have lived out his days skipping stones across the calm waters of the Baie des Chaleurs. From his contact with the Amerindians he had acquired a calm and gentle wisdom, like those fog banks that creep over the horizon at the dawn of day. But a terrorist political movement was threatening to overturn the Government of Quebec.

François, I can't sit still and watch what's going on at home now. I hear the hoarse voice of Revolution calling me across the forests of spruce. I'm coming, so watch for me!

I didn't need any help from him. I mean, governments come, governments go. Kidnapping. Blackmail. Police. Threats. Flattery. Taxes. Laws. Communiqués. Negotiations. It all happened on television between politicians and journalists. Jacques got pretty uptight too, of course. It didn't affect me, I was a delivery man for Jolicoeur Laundry and I had just as many shirts for washing whether there were soldiers all over the sidewalks or not. That's what Monsieur Rosen means when he says that trade is the stable element in a society.

Arthur highballed back to Montreal in his green Chevrolet tricked out inside with fishing lures stuck in the baize overhead. Gold spoons with black stripes, black spoons with orange spots, multi-coloured flies on steel hooks tied with whiskers and wild duck down, stuck all over, even on the visor, silver shot with vermilion, lures enough to bait all the fish in the rivers.

The minute he arrived he began getting his nose in the nation's business. Mind you, in Canada the nation's business is rather modest, like its population. We're taken up most with patchwork quilting. Which of the French, English or Indians have sewn the most pieces in our wondrous patchwork from sea to sea? Will the seams hold? A debate as old as Europe lives on in North America. Our patchwork quilts last forever. Geez!

I don't swear any more except if I hammer my thumb. I watch my language because a security man who invokes church vessels or body functions sounds coarse, that's what Jean-Charles told me on one of my first days. Funny, the Québécois aren't churchy any more but they still use a lot of churchy words. All the Americans have for swearing is sex. Fuck you! It's pretty limited, but it makes for strong dialogue. Fuck you! Cocksucker! It's virile—there are playwrights like David Mamet who make money hand-over-fist with three words, and that's a mouthful. To the last crumb! Arthur took the cake to the last crumb too but it wasn't with just a couple of words because Arthur's the king of con artists.

"I don't want you to call me Arthur. My real name is Nadja Astac. I've gone back to my roots. Maman was Huron, you know that because Grandmother came from Bersimis. Look at our nose, it's hooked, and there's no mistaking our cheekbones. Then our black hair ..."

"Arthur, Amerindians are beardless."

"Oh, you never get the point!"

The point I got mighty fast was that Arthur was raking in substantial sums of money to help his revolutionary pals stay ahead of the army and police. He'd found the right charitable circuit and the necessary arguments. Even Jacques, who's pretty tightfisted, gave him a thousand dollars. The line Arthur alias Nadja Astac was stringing was that his knowledge of Micmac would help him establish an underground in the Indian reservations on the American border. After that the boys would slip over to Cuba disguised as Iroquois, and bye-bye tracks. He stored the cash in shoeboxes on the floor of his Chevrolet, which he kept in the yard of my bungalow on Île Perrot, not far from the Mill Road. I had put the house up for sale, but the political uncertainty of this revolutionary period was bad for realties, my agent said.

A few terrorists were arrested and others slipped through the net laid for them, perhaps thanks to the great teacher-preacher Nadja Astac. We'll never know. Arthur, alias The Lobster, disappeared one fine morning. It must have been moulting time.

17. I think Arthur was on the right track. I saw an Eskimo grandmother on television who couldn't understand her grandson because he'd been brought up in English. It wasn't English that was to blame, it was injustice. I don't talk much about it because people think poor Arthur's soft in the head. They think we're all going to be speaking the same language, all singing to the same tune into the same mike in praise of homogeneity. No more shaking the bottle to mix up the cream. We're all going to be drinking skim. When my brother left it was to fight this dubious kind of harmony. I had no news of him till seven years later, never got a postcard, never a letter, not a single word, so I thought he was dead and buried along with those harebrained schemes of his.

It was human ecology more than oil-soaked birds that Arthur cared about. These years, dozens of nations disappear and hundreds of languages die out and neither Greenpeace nor the newspapers bat an eye. My brother didn't want us to have to create zoo-type ethnological parks where we'd keep the last specimens of the last Amazonian tribes alive behind bars. He was devoting himself to the service of endangered species, he said.

He phoned me one day out of the blue, as if I should have expected it. I was already living in Montreal and had been working at Bordeleau Transport for several months. Jacques and I had practically written off our Indian and forgotten him. Jacques had left television and was writing for *La Presse* but was still making notes for his novel. A bigger project than *War and Peace*, the way it was shaping up.

Arthur rattled on like a coffee mill, I couldn't stop him. He'd been wanting to come home, he said, but the "Canadians", meaning the RCMP, were watching him too closely.

"I've been making killings on the stock exchange," he told me, "that's why I can travel. Well, it's not that easy, but I've got brothers everywhere now."

"What about us?"

"You're my blood brothers, that's different. Listen François, I've got problems. The Mounties are getting in my way, you know. They've tried to kill me, too. I've got a bullet in my thigh to this day. But when you've had children die in your arms you stop backing off, there's too much suffering to give up the fight. I don't ask much for myself, just a "wam" at the bottom of a garden will do. I had that near Paris but a lousy journalist tried to do us in. A million! He wanted a million francs not to publish!"

I couldn't get much of what he was talking about of course. What *was* going on in my head was wondering if he was phoning from the Gobi Desert or Amsterdam or Boston. He didn't want to give me his number. He sounded as crystal-clear as if he was calling from next door.

"You never thought of calling me before tonight? Where are you hiding out, India or Toronto?" He was getting me on edge with his talk. "So what can I do for you?"

This brother who didn't call very often wanted me to get a passport ("You don't travel much") and send it to him. ("It's not much to ask and it'll save my life.") Nadja Astac knew I was a pushover. The Galarneau clan was not going to let its lost sheep down, wherever. I couldn't brush him off, we'd fought too many imaginary enemies together on hands and knees under the flowering lilacs. We were two little boys talking on the telephone, wreathed in mystery, like Batman and Robin.

"Figure a month at most, time to get the papers, photos, signature, then you can take it all to Ottawa, right?" You'd have thought he was Humphrey Bogart.

For the photo, Arthur suggested I do my hair the way Papa did when he went to sing at vespers. Papa used to be the star of the choir loft, *Domine, benedicere. Amen.* Between trips to Missouri I did as I'd promised. Souls of generosity can't refuse to help a neighbour in need. I'm not the go-away-don't-bother-me kind. I was even ready to deliver with my own hands if Arthur could get to the States so we could see each other.

I waited for him to call again as he'd said he would. A month, two months, then ten years went by, not to mention winters, without a sign of life from him. Since then, whenever I'm asked what he's doing I say he's living in San Francisco. Maman doesn't know he's disappeared. I invent tours and business ventures for him and his success makes her happy. She's even prouder of him than she is of Jacques and me.

"So Arthur's a millionaire, you say?"

"Yes, Maman, he's a philanthropist, even."

"A real Galarneau. I'm pleased one of you is devoting himself to humanity, François. Your father's going to be pleased too, but he's gone fishing, I'll tell him when he gets back."

Before I hang up I recite my lessons for her, I've found an old Latin grammar, Maman remembers some declensions and says I'm getting along well at school; I'd say that's obvious.

18. I told him when I arrived, as I put my bag on the unmade bed, I told him, "Jacques, you're a sucker to be living here!" I was puffing as hard as if I'd just run a marathon, and his sixth-floor walk-up studio-WC-kitchenette looked older than Canada.

"It's not bad for Paris, you know. It's even pretty nice. Pads are expensive. It's respectably furnished."

My brother had been in Paris since December. To him, the best thing going was a sixth-floor in the Sixth Arrondissement, around the corner from publishing houses, the Collège de France and the Sorbonne, in the shadow of the literary establishment with the ghosts of Sartre and Simone walking near the cafés and the probability of rubbing shoulders with Umberto Eco or Marguerite Duras in some neighbourhood bookstore. Everything in this holy city evoked literature and its creation and its history and mythology. Most of the books I'd ever read in my life had been written and published within shouting distance of Jacques's window.

"Picasso lived in the studio over there behind that wall, d'you see it?"

I saw it. Even the rooftops in Paris have a poetic air. The stones around me had been polished, kissed, bloodied, immortalized. I was going back in time without getting out of my depth. I found all of it at once fabulous and disturbing.

"You know, children go to Disneyland to meet their favourite characters like Mickey and Donald, and walk around in artificial streets where they see real sets from their favourite movies and hear songs from the TV programs they watch. Going to Disneyland is like living the dreams and breathing the stories of one's childhood."

We were standing side by side at the window, which was open wide. Invisible pigeons were cooing below us, the air was balmy even at noon, the light was golden, filtering through a light fog, and I couldn't help turning my eyes to a majestic dome in the distance. I knew that somewhere, not far away, famous writers were heading for bars that were just opening their doors.

"What's Mickey Mouse got to do with us?"

My brother's more educated than me but at times he's really thickheaded. Arriving in Paris unexpectedly to do something I'd set my heart on—I'd let him know only a few days before—I'd caught him in one of his particularly dense stages.

"What *I'm* seeing here are *my* favourite characters, writers living and dead and some even standing in squares as statues, and it doesn't matter much which because Tournier is my Mickey Mouse, Sollers is my Captain Hook, Butor is my Donald Duck, and the streets they gave me to see in their novels, the smells they brought me in their poetry and the buildings along these boulevards, Disneyland's pavilions if you will, all of it's a wonderful, artificial, make-believe world, pure fabrication—Literatureland, don't you see?"

Jacques stood with his hands in his pockets and listened to me talk, wearing the superior smile of a guy who knows you'll get over these starry-eyed outbursts brought on by the magic of the place. He must have been telling himself that the air of Paris was going to my head the way air bubbles do in a diver

45

who's let himself be taken too deep.

"That's not all there is, François. Before you go all gaga, we have to eat. And you're going to tell me about this marriage deal before you take the fatal plunge."

We went down to the street. I remember that long staircase, slightly tilted like the whole building, Tower of Pisa style, and the unspeakable smell of mould that got you by the throat the minute you went out onto the landing. Centuries of humanity had trudged back and forth by these walls, which had got downright mangy on some floors. You could see how Paris came to be famous for its funguses. In the space of only a few days I ran up four steps at a time in desperation, crept down gingerly in trepidation, staggered from one floor to the next, dragged myself up on my rear, counted the steps over and over, up and down, up and down, ten times, twenty times. But on that first afternoon, as I stood with my hand on my brother's shoulder, I had no idea that this staircase was going to be the principal witness of my shifting states of mind and spirit.

19. The restaurant was as smoky as a trench in the Great War. The diner on my left ate his soup with a cigarette dangling from his lips.

"What kind of people eat here?"

"Don't know really. Tourists, locals, journalists. Why?"

"D'you think Breton's hands held this menu, or that Aragon ordered this same pork *au parfum forestier?*"

"Cut out the hogwash. I'll send you on a guided tour,

Cocteau's shoemaker, Sartre's barber, Paulhan's house, Sagan's café, like a tour of movie-star hangouts in Beverly Hills. Is that what you're after?"

Plain to see, my brother hadn't grasped the depth of my emotion. It isn't every day that a fellow gets to walk around a city that's a living library. He raised his glass to my health and without answering I drank down two glassfuls one after the other.

"To your fiancée. Do I know her?"

I replied, "Wait, let me explain. My chief, Jean-Charles, spends a lot of time in ethnic restaurants. He says the only way Montreal has any taste is with curry, banana peppers or coriander. All he trusts are chopsticks and wooden skewers. I often go with him, so as the weeks go by we make friends or acquaintances, mostly with immigrants from all over the world who wait on table or work in the kitchens."

"What on earth can you find to talk about? People like that ..."

"If you've already got everybody pigeon-holed, what's the point of trying to explain anything?" Jacques is one of those tall, thin people who think they know it all. You can recognize them by the slightly stooped backs they get from poring over society's problems. They burn me up!

He looked at me a mite remorsefully. "Sorry, I'm listening."

"We have a drink together at the tavern in the mall or we go bowling, or sometimes play pool. It's very friendly and relaxed and bit by bit I've got interested in international politics. What would you like to know about strife in India, terrorism in Pakistan, refugee camps in Hong Kong or Latin-American dictators? Go ahead, ask me."

"I believe you."

"On pay day we play craps and make bets. But you

wouldn't be interested in that." Jacques could have kept quiet and let me let off steam but the red wine was making him sarcastic, I guess.

"So you won a bride at cards?"

"It happened when we were playing cards, but not that way. I met her brother Paulo first. We're about the same age. When he was a very small boy he immigrated to France from Cambodia with his family before moving on to try his luck in Montreal."

"You're going to marry a Cambodian?"

"Listen, Paulo is a super guy. Very appealing. I'm sure you'd like him." Then I lifted my empty glass and added, "Woo-oo, I'm drinking too fast, forgive me!"

It happened because the wine in Paris, even by the carafe, is nicer to drink than anything imported to Canada. I don't know what they do to the stuff we get, how they doctor it, maybe they add Gravol so it won't get seasick, but it's all the same whether it's sent in tankers that used to carry oil or already bottled-with-tender-loving-care-at-the-Château, it's never really smooth and the colour's never as rich as a cardinal's robe, or any of that. Jacques ordered a second bottle like the first. I was ready to forgive him anything.

"Did you know that Pol Pot, the head of the Khmers Rouges, studied here in Paris?"

"Must have been the philosophy that went to his head. Going to university isn't the be-all and end-all."

"I often think they should have turned the world over to our agency to guard."

"I can see it now: Harry Rosen, Secretary General of the United Nations! Was your friend Paulo wearing glasses?"

Jacques crams his head full of information. He knew what had happened to the intellectuals out there, how they'd all been killed, but he'd never really suffered himself. So I told him the story. Paulo's family were persecuted by Pol Pot and to save their skins had fled to the jungle eighty kilometres from Phnom Penh. Of course the Maoist-fascists kept after them so they fled even farther away, to a swampland. There were the parents and four children including Paulo. The father, Mr. Soon, had been a producer for national television. By day they hid and slept and by night they lived half-submerged in stagnant water with the air stinking of elephant fart and mosquitoes eating their eyelids, while they themselves nibbled on soft treebark and ate black-beetles and water spiders and whatever else they could catch. A rat was a banquet but the snakes that slipped by under their armpits were too quick to be feasible fare.

The father was the first to crack, after two months of wading in the swamp. The heat was unbearable on account of the humidity. And then all of them had spent too long in the swamp ooze. Fever. Fear. Mr. Soon drowned. The children found him face down one morning at sunup, swollen like a water skin, stiff as a log. Without a moment's hesitation the mother cut Mr. Soon in pieces and the family ate meat for ten days. From father-provider to father-provender.

Jacques turned steadily greener as I recounted Paulo's adventure. "It's an intellectual's story," I told him, "so it doesn't matter if it spoils a *pâté en croûte* for you."

I'd got the picture. In Paris, intellectuals often argue as if they just don't want to understand or even listen to each other. They attack, pour scorn and turn their backs on one another. They're intolerant. On TV I've seen film critics tear a film apart limb from limb, as if they had to have an arm to wolf down. It starts with principles and ends in swamp-rot.

49

20. What annoyed me about Paulo was that he wouldn't open a book. That's what got us talking at first; he had come to ask us if we wanted tea, we were in an Indian restaurant, and we said, "Sure," but Jean-Charles insisted on green tea and Paulo made a peculiar face. Jean-Charles got excited and said, "Is there something wrong with the tea?" So Paulo stepped back a pace and replied, "Excuse me, Boss, it's those books on your table there, they've made me feel sick. The tea's good. The books smell like death."

"What's that? My books *stink*?" We had a hell of a argument. There weren't many customers so Paulo would do some serving then come back to our table to carry on the discussion. In the end Jean-Charles invited him to come the following Monday, all three of us had the day off, for a little poker game at his apartment on Rue Esplanade across from the football field. Paulo was funny, he told French stories, I mean, ones he'd heard while he was in France, mostly dirty stories of course. He liked Montreal, he'd got seriously interested in National League hockey and had acquired a puck autographed by Mario Lemieux.

We came to be buddies, Paulo and I, and were practically inseparable. I thought he should start by reading Saint Ex, he really loved *Vol de nuit*, then more modern novels, *Le Salaire de la peur*, things like that. The problem was that my friend Paulo was lonesome for his family and spent a fortune on long-distance phone calls. When he won at cards he'd rush to the phone whatever the hour and call his younger sister.

"She's the girl I'm going to marry,"

"You mean you've never even *seen* her?"

"It's to help reunite families, our immigration law allows it. I'll marry her, bring her home with the papers, she'll be back with her brother, and that's it."

"François, you're out of your mind! These phony marriages aren't encouraged, they're punished by the law! Have you got a picture? May I see it?"

I've never seen Jacques so upset, except maybe when Radio-Canada turned down a television series he'd really done a lot of work on. He looked at me across the little table. We were elbow-to-elbow with our neighbours and he must have been wondering if they knew I was stark raving mad. I mean, this marriage *was* a risk. Catherine Soon was small and rather pretty in the photo, with just the smile to melt a security man's heart.

"Jacques," I said to him while he looked more closely at Paulo's sister, "the earth is small, we have to help each other."

"You're right, François, the earth is small. So they can get together without you. My advice is to let it drop. You can set yourself up at my place, you can see round Paris, you can go to the theatre, movies, the circus, whatever, there's a fantastic exhibition at the Grand Palais, I'll even buy you champagne at the Crazy Horse if I have to, but you're going to go home the way you came, free and happy."

"What if it's love at first sight?"

Naturally, Jacques reminded me of impetuous decisions I'd made before, the bus when I was twenty, Marise, the Institute and my wanting to escape. I didn't bite. It was the future I was thinking about, the one you can see ahead at forty, when the neck of the funnel starts getting tighter.

21. I slept like a log. The red wine, the jet lag, the excitement. When I opened my eyes there were cracks in the

ceiling. I'd have to warn Catherine that I snore like a snow-mobile at times. Jacques must have gone to write in the back room of some carefully chosen bistro, he's an arithmomaniac, Dr. Staetdler explained to me, if he doesn't follow a routine he can't keep up with his work. It's different with me.

I wanted to telephone my fiancée, Paulo had told her I was coming, but there was no phone in the room. The one in the booth at the corner of the street only worked with a card. The nit-pickers were out to get my goat! I wandered about aimlessly. I was paralyzed by the first phone I'd approached and I was seeing this city for the first time! Paris smelled strongly of diesel exhaust, urine, tobacco and printer's ink.

Here and there at a streetcorner I'd see a man sitting with an upturned hat at his feet; I'd leave him a franc, saying, "It's not much but it's from the heart." A couple of bums under a porch held out a bottle to me. I was sorry I wasn't wearing my uniform with the planet and lightning logo so they'd know someone was watching out for them. Beggars in Paris are older than they are in Montreal. It's a young country we live in, you don't have to wait till you're fifty to sleep in the Métro.

At Garland we're supposed to kick out winos and beggars. Only authorized agents of charitable organizations are allowed to hold out their hands. Direct contact with poor people, who aren't always clean, would upset the mall's ecology. So Centraide, Red Feather, Red Cross and Bn'ai Brith have rationalized the beneficence of shoppers. I've advised my men not to be dumb when a bum shows up, to buy him a donut and coffee, explain the situation and show him back to the exit. After all, there are premises where poverty is out of place, the Garland Mall, Disneyland and Literatureland for instance.

22. The next day Jacques bought me a telephone card, it had a picture of Fats Waller the jazz singer on it. This telecard was one of a series. Jacques told me not to throw it away when I'd used all the calls because there are crazies who collect them. This is a country of fleamarkets. In ours we collect baseball or hockey cards that smell of chewing gum. To think our ancestors came out of their caves and invented the wheel just to come to this!

Catherine invited me for a meal. On the telephone she had a French accent, which was disconcerting. I'd expected her to have a lisp or something, because of Cambodia. We all give away where we're from by our speech, even the Parisians, who talk with their tongues glued to their palates if they're from Paris proper, or to the backs of their throats if it's the suburbs. I talk through my nose, I know. Catherine told me everything was ready for the wedding. I was kind of nervous but I was gallant and said my brother had seen her picture and thought she was very pretty.

I spent all afternoon looking for a gift to take her the next day. I wasn't going to turn up with a can of maple syrup. I haggled for some jewelry but the prices were out of sight. Thinking of Maman, I looked in the *confiseries*; stepping inside one of these places was like suddenly lifting the lid off a box of Black Magic after tearing through the cellophane.

Jacques advised me to take her flowers. "People do that a lot here, and besides, in this situation it's you who's the gift." He asked me not to promise anything or sign anything. He was afraid I was going to get hornswoggled.

23. The sun was radiant, it was mid-April and there were leaves on the trees and flowers everywhere. Montreal had been awash in slush when I'd left—there's no justice! On the other hand, I took it for granted that Galarneau should be along. In Villejuif I got lost before finding the address between two machine shops. An enormous gold-yellow tomcat sitting on the roof of a trailer in the yard in front didn't even turn his head when I opened the garden gate. I rang the bell, I was as nervous as all get-out, and introduced myself, presenting my bouquet. Catherine put her nose in the flowers and smiled nicely, gave me a little bow, held out her hand, then her cheeks, I didn't know what I should kiss.

We talked about her brother. There was more flesh on her than in the photo, I don't know what she thought of me. I'd given my hair a daub of wet look to make myself classier.

"Welcome, *monsieur le cow-boy canadien*," she said with a smile, then put her hand over her mouth as if to hide her teeth. I know now that this is a polite kind of oriental custom. It wasn't the right time to explain what "cowboy" meant, so I just let that go.

I stepped into a big room, a sort of kitchen-living-room-family-room. Something was simmering on the stove and the windows behind the bamboo curtains were fogged up. Nondescript wall-to-wall on the floor. Not *The Arabian Nights*. I counted eight places set on an immaculate tablecloth; the table in the middle of the room filled all the space there was. Catherine showed me to the only armchair, a kind of wooden throne facing the TV. On top of the TV there was incense smoking before a jovial, pot-bellied Buddha. Jean-Charles had a serious rival in this fellow. The little altar intrigued me, I wanted to ask whether they kept ancestors' ashes in the red jar or the black dish, then I remembered the

54

father and didn't like to ask.

There was a long silence. Catherine kept standing before me; the only voice was the pot on the stove murmuring I don't know what. I nearly suggested turning on the TV. It's not always easy to find the right opening, I mean, even when you're engaged. I hesitated to take her in my arms. Then I waved at the set table and looking around toward the door said exactly what was in my head: "Are we expecting friends?"

"Oh no," she said, "just the immediate family. They won't be long. We wanted all of us to be together to celebrate our leaving."

She was almost clapping her hands together like a little girl. I thought to myself, There's going to be feeling in this marriage, not just convenience.

"It's *hyper sympa*, François," she said in Parisian jargon meaning she thought it exceedingly kind, "to agree to help us in this way. All of us are very grateful to you, *beginning with my fiancé.*"

My first reaction was to smile like someone who has just swallowed too big a mouthful and then my diaphragm cut loose. Nervousness, surprise, fatigue, jet lag. The absurdity. I laughed until tears came and Catherine, caught up in my mirth, laughed with me. She managed to say, "Would you like a drink while we wait?" I had a drink, with ice, then several more in too rapid succession. She went back to her cooking pots while I raised my glass to Buddha, asking him to tell me I'd heard wrong. But the paunchy idol just kept on laughing, for the family arrived one after another, beginning with the fiancé, an evil-looking Hungarian with a clean-shaven face, a cheerful front, green in his eye, a mop of curly hair and a polka-dot tie at his neck. Then Catherine's children, whom she introduced proudly, three boys and two girls. Pierre, the eldest, was pleased to meet me he affirmed as he shook my hand, though he did not wish to emigrate; he had a job, a girl-friend, wheels, and plans in which Canada did not figure. The others, Éric, fourteen, Joachim, six, Marianne, twelve, and Maude, nine, were all coming with us. The fiancé was reckoning on using Pierre's papers, which ought to take care of the only snag. Good old Paulo!

I told myself I'd leave right after dessert. The children were good-looking, bright-eyed and cheery, and the youngest, Joachim, attached himself to me then and there. He kept calling me "*tonton*", meaning "uncle", though I would have rather it be "Papa". I think I was the only one who knew I hadn't known how things were. We sat down at the table with Catherine on my right, the preposterous fiancé on my left and the children arranged around us as if for a family portrait. They had pulled out all the stops, lots of different little dishes, and ambrosial wine as well. I didn't always know what I was eating, Barbary duck or offal, but it was damn good! I found my tongue after the fourth round of a fabulous bordeaux. I was the uncle from America, full of tales of adventure, flush with money and kindly thoughts and ready to say anything it took to tickle the little folk from the old country.

I wasn't the one who suggested Niagara Falls for the honeymoon, with its promenade, slide shows, mists and fog and motels. The famous falls are the stuff of dreams, even in Paris. They adorn the façades of tourist agencies that serve up America in landscape slices: Arizona, Malibu Beach, craggy Rocky Mountains, wheat-covered Prairies, barren Tundra, never a living soul or a lived-on street; it's vast open spaces they sell. But when Niagara came up I suggested the fiancé should go over the falls in a barrel. "It's a real American adventure, you know. The barrel's metal with a thick foam lining and they close it up like a jar of pickles and drop you in the water upstream."

He looked at me aghast.

"Go on, there's no danger in it. Living in Montreal's more dangerous, there's a mugger behind every tree, while in the barrel everything's calm and peaceful—the current surrounds you, the barrel spins gently like a squirrel cage, and by the time it comes to the brink of the falls it's already got up a head of steam and can't possibly, *absolutely* can't crash on the rocks right below—unless something goes wrong." The children clamoured to hear more. Turning to Joachim who was all ears I added more softly, "The critical moment comes once over the brink, when the barrel plummets into the dark, seething waters, ten, twelve feet deep—three, four metres. Will it rise again or stay below? Will it bob up all covered with foam or will it nosedive, take in water and stay down for ever? That's the way America judges whether a man's a man or not. If you don't do the barrel trip on your honeymoon, you're not."

I thought to myself that I was being rash and crossed my fingers under the table. A Harry Sécurité man doesn't lie; on occasion he exaggerates.

"It's kind of symbolic, a honeymoon, you know," the fiancé was telling the children. Your mother and I have been together three years, so ..."

"So what?"

"So I'm not going in the barrel."

"Then how are you going to guide their studies and advise them when things get tough? They won't have a father if you don't go over the falls in a barrel!"

I was pretty smashed. Catherine kept pouring me wine, I've never known how to drink, I kept emptying the glass but she stepped in before I got aggressive. The kids, she told me, weren't all of the same father. Pierre and Éric were from her first marriage and the three others were the luck of the draw. Yet it spoke wonders for genetics and a mother's love that all of them, though of different colourings, had the same eyes, the same chin and the same winning smile.

"So, Catherine, we'll get married and your fiancé will be my son for a while?"

"Long enough to check in at the consulate then get by the immigration officer," the temporary son said. "I'll cut my hair, shave off my moustache, buy me a pair of basketball boots—I'm not any bigger than Pierre—and wear jeans, that should do it, shouldn't it?"

Many-faced, as flexile as a jellyfish, capable of switching on any accent, the fiancé was engaged in selling roses in the restaurants of Montmartre and the Champs-Élysées, with the two little girls in tow to soften up the tourists. Maude (she was nine but looked seven) recited for me, "Monsieur, if you don't buy a flower from me I'll have to sell my body in order to eat." Everyone laughed. "That even gets to the eggheads," sonny-boy said to me in a knowing aside. By the time desert came, a charlotte russe, I still didn't like his face but I'd decided I'd have to put up with him. I'd promised Paulo I'd bring Catherine home with me and I'd agreed to a marriage of convenience and I wasn't going to go back on my word.

The sonny-boy-fiancé gave me a cigarillo, which I didn't light. I chewed on it to keep me awake as I answered questions from the children, who wanted to know all about Montreal, what it would be like there, what kind of house they were going to, how cold it would be—I got muddled in centigrade degrees but promised I'd teach them to skate. To the question "What's your job?" I answered, feeling pleased with myself and looking the fiancé in the eye, "I'm in the security forces." I thought I was impressing him. He jumped up, knocking his chair over, and came and kissed me on both cheeks, men do that to each other in Europe, it's not as pansy as it is here.

"That's great!" he exclaimed, "I always need protection in my profession. I'm glad, François." Then he poured me coffee and a liqueur while Catherine swept up the baguette crumbs and cleared the table.

The children were in front of the TV, it was one of those airhead game-shows that we're seeing more and more of on ABC or NBC or even out of Montreal, with cable I never can tell where they come from. This one was done by the French but with the usual setup. Three girls, three boys, a blind date, destination unknown. Seeing as how a blind date was the way I met Marise, I could have told them a thing or two, only here the M.C. was being smart-alecky, making remarks you could take three ways. The prize was a weekend for two, all included, I didn't hear the end. The boys kept saying, "Yeah, great, yeah, all right!" and the girls, "Hey, how's that, eh!"

I glanced at the papers Catherine brought me and the forms from City Hall, but I was too plastered to read and understand it all and sign on the dotted line so I got up and gave hugs all round and left with the papers.

They wanted to drive me home in the fiancé's Peugeot, which must have smelled all flowery like a hearse.

"I'll take the Métro," I told them, "It's my first trip to Paris and I like your trains." I needed to get my head in order. I leaned it against the dirty window and watched the city's guts go by, they were as dark as intestines where Galarneau never shines, and my ears were filled with the screech of the wheels on the rails.

24. My biological clock was playing tricks on me. I woke at two in the morning, lying on the mattress that Jacques

59

had unrolled between the table and an electric radiator. The neighbourhood smelled of French fries, crêpes and beer, and four floors below us a blues band was spinning out the night in a private club. Through a corner of the window, which the curtain was too short to cover properly, I counted the chimneys silhouetted against the skyline. Eaves-roosting pigeons were providing background noise. I should have got out of bed and picked up a book but I stayed put and tried to get to sleep, succeeding only as day was breaking. When I finally woke again, my mouth was foul and my eyes felt full of sand, it was late morning already, and Jacques had gone out to write with a *demi* on the table in front of him. I drank a café-au-lait standing up at the first counter I came to, it's cheaper than on a terrace, then went looking for Jacques.

I was particularly edgy and anxious that morning. Should I phone Montreal? Paulo, Jean-Charles and the guys had pooled their savings and sent me on a mission that had since taken on a different colour. I'd promised to bring Catherine back with me, but did I really have to go through with this phony marriage? Did the whole tribe have to come too? I didn't know what to think any more.

I found my brother in a neon-lit establishment on the Place de l'Odéon. He was sitting with his back to a bevelled and flowered mirror in which were reflected the merry faces of a dozen Japanese. Jacques saw me coming but remained seated, open-mouthed as if suddenly struck with paralysis. There was a newspaper spread out in front of him, hiding his manuscript.

"I hope I'm not interrupting your inspiration."

"It doesn't matter," he replied with a dazed look on his face, "reality has outdone my fiction." Then he placed his finger on a picture in the upper right quadrant of page three in *France-Soir*. "Somebody had left this paper on the banquette. I started looking through it. It must be fate. I'm *flabeurgasté!*"

My brother doesn't use many anglicisms. He even belongs to an association for the promotion of the French language which awarded him its annual grand prize in the salons of the Montreal Saint-Jean-Baptiste Society. I realized at once that he wasn't joking. *Flabeurgasté!* I grabbed the paper, my hands trembling with emotion. Adrenalin, gallons of adrenalin, swept though me from my scalp to the soles of my feet. Now I too was flushed and excited.

"Do you see what I see?" Jacques asked. "D'you recognize that Indian?"

The camera doesn't lie. Between two plain-clothes police officers, his beard still long, wearing a radiant, arrogant smile and across his forehead a head-band with beaded geometric figures, Arthur seemed to be mocking us. I looked at Jacques, chewing my lips. My brain was jigging as if microwaved. Jacques put up his hand and ordered two cognacs. It wasn't yet noon! I ordered two more: it's always noon somewhere in the world.

The caption under the picture read, "A Canadian guru is arrested in Brussels." Arthur was not getting very good press, it must be said. He'd been arrested coming out of an up-scale restaurant and booked for fraud, counterfeiting, passing counterfeit bills, and corruption of minors. Meanwhile, I thought to myself, his youngest sibling is about to contract a marriage of convenience aggravated by corruption of identity. A fine, upstanding family! The Indian had a criminal record in France, we read. He was known by several aliases, including Brother Amadeus, Nadja Astac and John O'Donnell. Dear Arthur! Passing himself off as a man of the church, a Micmac or an Anglo had opened all doors to him. He was operating a European natural foods business. Interpol had been tailing him and the Belgian police had nailed him.

After the cognac came uncertainty. We were crushed by the news and didn't know what to do. Then, once the alcohol had warmed the blood in our veins, our doubts vanished. It all seemed like a message intended especially for us. Arthur was counting on us, it was written in the stars and printed in this newspaper.

"I'll keep believing he's innocent till he pleads guilty," I said.

"It's you who's innocent, *mon pauvre* François." Jacques tore the page out of the newspaper and folded it neatly. "Arthur's a crook. He was already one at twenty, remember. We both know he's a phony Indian. As for the bit about minors, I don't think that's like him ..."

Jacques was putting up a good front, but I sensed that he was deeply shaken by this business. I told Catherine that we would be away for a few days and not to change her plans in any way, that I accepted the situation, but that for the moment I had a family to stitch back together too.

25. Paris-Brussels can be done by streetcar, or almost. A train leaves every two hours, so that same evening Jacques and I ate in a tourist trap around the corner from La Grande Place. The girls and the French fries were all blonde. Jacques said, "What d'you suppose they'd say if they knew the Hot Dog King was in town, and one of his brothers is the Micmac King, and I'm the Beer King?"

In Quebec we never had the French Revolution. The aristocracy went home and got bumped off there. As a result

62

we still have a soft spot for royalty, the proof is, the Queen of England is still our sovereign. "Might she come and live with us when we're sovereign too?" But Jacques didn't want to hear any more about politics. He was drinking like a bottomless barrel, partly because we were eating steamed clams but also because he was ashamed to have Arthur hauled into court. I wasn't exactly feeling smug either.

Walking back to the hotel, we passed the restaurant where Nadja Astac had been arrested. Our brother hadn't done the hard-core gangster bit and shot up the place with a machine gun, so of course as news goes the whole thing was already forgotten. A helpful passer-by pointed out the police station, Central Division, behind the Hotel Amigo on a small street of the same name. Together, we brothers felt brave enough to go and make enquiries then and there, but Jacques really had drunk too much and I suggested strongly that we come back early in the morning, with clear heads and empty stomachs.

Jacques was no sooner in bed than he was snoring like a rummy. I wasn't sleepy but lay still on my back with my hands crossed over my chest, like a knight on top of his tomb. Too many things were charging about in my brain. I saw us running with our bags through the gloom of the station to buy tickets, then to the train on Track 59. From the train window we'd seen walls covered with graffiti as if we were passing through New York, and abandoned factories with cold chimneys and yards nothing but mud. Then freight cars from the forties with grotty brown tarpaulin roofs. Had they been used for transport to the camps? Were they being left on these sidings to stand as monuments to human cruelty?

While my brother read the daily newspapers, the *Herald Tribune*, *Le Monde*, I in my own way was discovering Europe, seeing it go by beyond the train windows like a continuous charcoal sketch. And I remembered, as we raced past red-brick towns, their houses supporting each other mutually, that Arthur Rimbaud had walked these highways, crossed these crossroads, seeking freedom that was absolute and filled with light. Arthur. Nature. Why had my brother come here to pose as an Indian? You'd have expected the opposite, a Belgian going to Arizona. Did Nadja Astac fancy himself an Amerindian ambassador? In Europe they've had a soft spot for Redskins ever since Columbus and Cartier brought a few back to melt the hearts of their queens. But those Redskins died of misery, didn't they? What would a Brussels cell be like? And what if we were taken for accomplices?

I think I dozed off as the three Galarneau brothers were being paraded before the international press in La Grande Place in Brussels. We were standing on a raised platform, hobbled and in chains and as naked as newborn babes. We had feathers in our hair and shells around our ankles, and a witch came forward wanting to marry me. She wore a fiendish smile and her hands reached toward my balls, itching to add them to the steaming stew of insects and swamp snakes simmering over a bamboo fire behind her.

26. The next morning we arrived at the Rue des Quatre Bras where stands the monumental Palais de Justice, which was inaugurated by King Leopold II. The architect's name was engraved in the stone, I don't recall what it was but I remember that the Flemish word for architect was *bouwmeester*, I liked it and thought at once of boom-town, the gold rush, the Klondyke, none of which have anything to do with architects;

it's just that I seem to be making more and more word associations by sound these days. It makes me think I ought to try rhyming with Maman to help her get back names she's lost. Considering no one knows whether losing one's memory is an illness or a ritual or just rust in the pipes.

My head was mush, Jacques was handling all this better than I was. He'd taken his time and nursed his beer. We'd walked from the hotel to the Place du Sablon where all the trades have costumed representatives, holding the tools of their crafts and perched on columns like turkeycocks. We did a tour of the park but I wasn't with it. I was reflecting that Monsieur Rosen, who's rich and cultivated, ought to make a gift to the city of Brussels, a modest statue, on a pedestal, of a security guard wearing the Harry Sécurité uniform and holding a book in his hand. The park would be safer. Besides, while big marble or plaster Saint Peters holding a guardian's keys can be seen in lots of Catholic churches, this would be the first lay tribute to our profession.

"In French fries you're the king; in security you behave like the pope. You never do anything by halves, François!"

I explained to Jacques, as we climbed the steep slope of the Rue de la Régence toward the courthouse, that although I was forcing myself to play a role in society these days, it didn't come naturally. "I'm more the Jack Kerouac type, you've heard of him?"

Jacques knew the Franco-American through his books of course, he'd even talked to him on the phone one day in preparation for a television interview. My brother knows too many people. His head must be like a railway station concourse, full of booming echoes, small futile voices, and faces glimpsed and as quickly forgotten.

We arrived opposite the columns of the Temple of Justice, which stood upon two tiers of stone that served no one any purpose. We entered through doors that dwarfed us before the Goddess. Now we were in an immense, gloomy hall dotted with theatrically lit tables, and around which lawyers and their clients whispered furtively. A large crowd was milling around and blocking the corridor leading to the Chambre des Enquêtes, the criminal investigation courtroom. We got the idea that these people were on the warpath. It was clearly Arthur's scalp they were after.

Jacques spotted a journalist and introduced himself as a reporter and me as a photographer. The Belgian wanted to know if the Indian was famous in Canada. We smiled politely. "In Canada there are several thousand Indians getting themselves noticed," Jacques said. "I think notoriety is easier on this side of the Atlantic."

While the two reporters palavered, I drifted slowly away to mingle with the crowd of plaintiffs who were after Arthur's hide. They were from all over, Amsterdam, Lille, Paris, there was even an old couple from Milan, as frail and brittle as icicles in April, who had come with their granddaughter. Corruption of minors? Each of the older people had a youngster—child, nephew, grandson—whom Nadja Astac had beguiled and persuaded to join his tribe.

Two former members were appearing as witnesses for the prosecution, a skinny boy and a small, thin girl with stiff, strawlike hair braided in a pitiful little pigtail at the back of her neck. "All they got to eat was thistle broth, monsieur!" I knew Arthur was a dud at cooking but the loathing these people bore for my brother could be smelled at a distance, like garlic. Had Nadja Astac been trying to teach the Europeans to live off Nature? The boy was especially vehement. He'd been made to work for months on end, miserably clothed and fed, preparing herbs that the Indian resold on the natural-foods market.

I felt a pang of envy when I heard that Arthur had opened some thirty vegan stores across the length and breadth of Europe. It made me think of my American dream, my hot-dog stands across the length and breadth of Quebec. Instead of capital, Arthur had a labour force paid in spiritual currency. He was The Brains. In my plan for a chain of restaurants, all I'd been was the King of Assholes.

In answer I just nodded and murmured, "How sad!" because I knew my brother really believed in his plants and trees and insects. So as not to harm animals, he'd never eaten a scrap of meat since he'd been six. "You don't change the order of nature on a whim," he used to say. "Before the Micmacs cut down a even a spruce tree, they ask the tree to forgive them." That morning in Brussels it was a Micmac that people intended to cut down.

We were all ushered into the courtroom, very white and cut by tall windows with varnished oak frames. You'd have thought you were in a chapel. The magistrates' table was set; they were going to be eating guru.

When Arthur arrived there was a murmur that sounded like a flock of wild birds taking off. Our Indian was pale-faced and wore a checkered lumberjack-shirt, which was fashionable in Paris at the time. They took off the handcuffs he was wearing. Nadja Astac was playing a role, I think; he kept putting on pensive airs and striking lordly poses to impress the court. As the session began and the Belgian crown prosecutor flapped his gown, I coughed and tried to catch Arthur's eye, but he remained expressionless, holding his head high and gazing into the distance.

From everything that was said at the courthouse that morning, I gathered that the Galarneaus were geniuses. Jacques himself poked me in the ribs now and then to stress our natural brother's imagination, the same imagination that he'd used in the games we played as children and then had put to the service of Montreal's cardinal for a number of years. All by himself, Arthur had dreamed up a truly great adventure, the Greatest Scientific Experiment in the History of Humanity. And he was being reviled for it! A sixteen-year project! The Great Homecoming March! The documents submitted showed that at the time it began he had garnered the support of almost every journalist in Paris. The March, on foot, was to be a tour of the world in five thousand, eight hundred and eighty days. It was in tune with the times. It was even sponsored in a vague kind of way by Captain Cousteau, the one you often see at sea on TV, and also by Alain Bombard and Paul-Emile Victor, who were celebrities although I'd never heard of them. It was a grand idea—the modern-day crusaders were setting off from their reserve on the outskirts of Paris to tour the world and return to their point of departure on the first of January of the year 2000. Véronique would have loved it, I'm sure she would have joined them. Arthur had always been an admirer of Jules Verne. He knew exactly how to give his projects a mythical dimension.

In a loud, Liège-accented voice, the prosecutor read an excerpt from the press release signed by Nadja Astac. "The ultimate aim of the March is to take a cartographical, culinary, botanical and sociological inventory of the planet Earth." In the age of satellites, yet! A magnificent thumb to the nose! It was to be a rigorous scientific pilgrimage. Before the second millenium began, the troupe would collect samples of various soils and chart the habitats of humanity, thus to produce a living, three-dimensional encyclopedia. The marchers would go from Europe into Africa and then cross Asia and return via Russia. I knew why Arthur was avoiding the Americas, it was because the Mounties were waiting for him. His brother Amerindians, he declared, could supply all the samples and documents the researchers needed to complete their work.

All this prelude, of course, was to demonstrate how my brother had hoaxed the marchers and journalists.

A lawyer called the little pigtail to the witness box. Arthur smiled as he looked at her but she kept her head turned away from him. She spoke in a faint little voice. "When we set off," she said, "there were nearly two hundred of us, women, men and children, with packs on our backs, a refrigerated truck ahead to keep our samples in and a bio-bus following for lab experiments."

"And who financed the project?"

"We weren't paid. I don't know."

"How old were you when the March began?"

"Twenty. I'd been two years in training. I'd studied mineralogy and survival. We had to be responsible and able to look after ourselves."

"Did Monsieur Astac accompany you?"

"He came and went. He was in charge of all the organization."

"Were you away a long time?"

"I marched for four years, then I got sick."

The ecological crusaders were dressed like East-Coast Amerindians, with Franciscan-type sandals and their hair in braids. They all spoke several languages learned during the preparation period. On the March they covered only a short distance each day and camped like gypsies. Châteaus and wigwams.

"We followed ancestral routes. The routes of humanity's great migrations."

I was stupefied.

The skinny boy came next. The beginning of the March, he said, was covered enthusiastically in the press and on television. But when the venture fell apart, the journalists who had praised the guru to the skies turned on him the more savagely. The March was brought to a halt in Morocco, then marooned in Ceuta, across the strait from Gibraltar. There were problems of territorial sovereignty, religion and money, and no one knew what would be next. The boy declared that Nadja Astac had abandoned his followers in the most abject poverty, that tuberculosis had broken out among them, and that grief-stricken parents had appealed to the Red Cross to bring them home.

That had been three years ago, and the Indian had been found only now. He must be made to pay!

A teepee in the rain was all that was left of the Amerindian dream in Europe.

27. The Chambre des Enquêtes sat only in the morning. After a ham sandwich washed down with a *Mort subite* beer at the Waterloo Tavern around the corner, Jacques and I went to the police, determined to see our brother. He was being held at Saint-Gilles Prison, not the Central Division station. The officer suggested we write him a note, which he would have delivered that very day. Since Arthur claimed to be a Micmac and we were insisting his name was in fact Galarneau, it was our word against his. Jacques wrote the letter. He's very fast in such circumstances.

I was rather overwhelmed by what was going on. I would have given a lot that day to find myself back at the Garland Mall, which must have been just opening its doors in that other time zone.

We told Arthur where we could be reached, I mean, we gave him our telephone number at the hotel, he'd be the one to decide if and when. I really would have liked to have had him at my wedding. It was dreaming in Technicolor, of course, but why settle for black and white? When Jacques went back to the hotel to wait for the call, I decided to go and see a movie. Movie houses are as empty as churches in the afternoon and the red velvet seats are soothing. So I settled into a seat as deep as an old sofa and watched a life of Van Gogh. I'd read and seen other lives of Van Gogh, but this was a French film and pretty special, with Dutronc scrawnier than Kirk Douglas in the American version. With his passion for yellow sunflowers, I said to myself, mightn't Van Gogh be a Dutch cousin, a Galarnogh? In the end, everything in his life went bad—the ear, the madness, his brother Theo in Paris, yet Vincent has left a legacy that people fight over today, even as far away as Japan.

I have a lot of trouble getting out of a film. I go into a theatre as François Galarneau, but when it's over I find myself out on the sidewalk in the skin of the hero. Perhaps I might never have gone back to being a Harry Sécurité agent if it weren't for a handful of punks coming in my direction. When I saw them with their Iroquois haircuts and chains round their hips, I crossed my arms and stood tall, and they made do with kicking garbage cans on their way by. If Van Gogh had been alive today, he'd have painted a punk with purple hair and a yellow sun on his shirt, sitting on a chair, as desperate as Vincent himself.

28. Jacques was waiting for me, leaning on the hotel bar, looking half asleep over his whiskey. There was a western showing on the television in the corner, it was *How the West Was Won*, I think, because I'd already seen those wagons. I took the remote control and surfed over to the news. In yellow on grey, along with other news, we read, "The Brussels police deplore the escape today of Nadja Astac, also known as the Indian, from Saint-Gilles Prison. Anyone having information regarding this matter is requested to contact …" I don't remember the telephone number. Jacques was furious. "D'you know what that means?" Of course I did.

I clicked back to the western, to a horseman galloping away across the prairie. "D'you s'pose that's Arthur?" I said.

Jacques was not amused. He doesn't really have a sense of humour, it's a sense of duty he's got. Fuming, he emptied his glass and sucked noisily on an ice cube. "We're screwed. We're not going to stick around Brussels just to watch the tarts go by!" He scratched the ear Vincent had cut off earlier in the afternoon.

"D'you think Arthur got our message before getting his ass out of there?"

"François! How am I supposed to know?"

"Maybe he's trying to find us."

"Well, the police thought of that before you did. Look out there, across the street."

I went to a window and with the back of my hand lifted the edge of the curtain slightly. There were indeed three men in a car, smoking and gazing at the sky. I moved back toward Jacques. "You know, I really loved that film on the Dutchman's passion."

"What difference does that make?"

"No difference. D'you think a person can die from beauty?"

"You can die from lots of things."

"I mean, can you be so sensitive and so hurt by all the ugliness round you that one day something beautiful literally takes your breath away?"

Jacques didn't answer. I was thinking of Arthur and marvelling at how far he'd come.

"D'you think he'd be in this mess if Quebec had been independent by now?"

"That's a theoretical question." Jacques wasn't in the mood for talking politics.

"He'd have devoted himself to the society and wouldn't have pretended to be an Amerindian. We wouldn't be sitting here frustrated like this."

"It's still a theoretical question."

"So what are we going to do about Arthur?"

"Nothing. We'll leave tomorrow. We're screwed, that's the way it is."

Then he ordered another whiskey, just like a real writer. Lucky for him he's not a security guard or an airplane pilot or a commander of a NATO strategic force. Alcohol makes you reckless. If there's one thing Monsieur Rosen won't forgive, it's one of his men drinking on the job. But I was on forced leave and wasn't going to let my brother get high all by himself. The barman got the drift.

"How's your book coming?" I said

"So-so."

He told me it was a love story that goes bad, based on an experience of his own. That's not my kind of book. I gave him some encouragement though, I mean, libraries are where you can learn about loving. The big problem today is that women read love stories and men read do-it-yourself books. So of course ...

29. Did we ever drink! The whole Atlantic Ocean! Then we went and sobered up with a piece of pizza in the park next door. The night was very dark and our faces were bathed by a cold Scotch mist. Jacques would laugh over nothing, then scare himself imagining the police stalking us behind the bushes.

Waiting for us at the desk when we got back to the hotel was an envelope with a radiant sun drawn on it. It contained a headband sewn with glass beads, blue, white and black. Jacques said, "Arthur's sent you his wedding present." That's all there was, not even a calling card. Indians are unpredictable.

I said, "Is your book like real life or the opposite?"

"Or the opposite."

"And in real life, what happens?"

"We go back to Paris, you're getting married on Saturday."

30. Monsieur Rosen was waiting for us at Mirabel Airport with Paulo, naturally, and Jean-Charles, Salem, Olivier and Tatsuro. Not all restaurants are closed on Sunday so the others were at work.

Catherine was wearing a black straw boater with a pink ribbon. On the lapel of her suit she had an antique pin given her by Istvan, her Hungarian fiancé, and in her hand a leather suitcase, my wedding present, a marvellous find made of pigskin that I'd discovered in the Galeries Lafayette. I must have looked like an aviator who's just left the controls of his plane. I still had on the new uniform I'd worn for the ceremony at the Villejuif City Hall, with the cap Jacques had bought for me at Le Vieux Campeur on the Rue des Écoles, the same blue as my suit. A happy Lindbergh of the Earth and Lightning Bolt.

I don't know whether my gang, noses pressed to the glass of the first-floor observation area, realized right off that the wedding party included the five children clutching multicoloured tote bags (counting the fiancé, youthened for the occasion), but once the administrative formalities and the customs and police checks were over, when the sliding doors had slid with that clicking sound, I saw several pairs of incredulous, questioning eyes. Paulo rushed to Catherine, who was crying for joy, and they embraced with great feeling. It was pretty damn touching to see them gaze at each other like children that way, and I cried too.

Jean-Charles and then all the others shook my hand, and I made the introductions the best way I could, I mean, that's not my department, so I took my wife's hand and said, "Here now, Catherine's going to introduce the family to you. I think you're going to get your money's worth." My guys clapped as each of the children was introduced wearing a big smile, even Istvan the fiancé who raised his hands over his head like a boxer grandstanding in the ring. For a while bedlam took the place of any conversation, then Salem led the boys off down the moving sidewalk to the garage.

We left the airport for the city in a procession. The Grand Homecoming parade. Monsieur Rosen's limousine led the way while in the other cars those skunks my buddies yakked about what I'd got myself into. We'd stacked our baggage in the van from the Drolet Street store, which Tatsuro was driving. The children were spread around in the first cars and I brought up the rear with Paulo and Jean-Charles. Catherine had got into the limo with the boss.

"François, I swear on the head of the Buddha my sister never said anything about children."

"You're lying, Paulo."

"She *never* said anything about the Hungarian."

"There I'm prepared to believe you."

"They're cute, aren't they?"

"You thought maybe it was time for me to start a family at my age?"

"I can't take them in with me. What are we going to do?"

Paulo lived in a one-and-a-half in a rundown building on De Maisonneuve Street. We had talked about renting another one in the same inn for Catherine, but this was out of the question now. Jean-Charles just had two rooms and a kitchen. "I'll take your wife's fiancé if you like," he said. He was making fun of his best friend. As we drove to the city on the Laurentian Autoroute, we talked over problems you never find in books. The agent of the Earth and Lightening Bolt had outdone himself.

"We've got a lot of mouths to feed."

"That's my problem," Paulo declared, lighting a cigarette which he quickly put out again when Jean-Charles glared daggers at him.

"Good. So you'll look after the shopping?" I knew Paulo would bet his last dollar on the weather before he'd buy us a can of peas.

"Couldn't the fiancé do his bit? He's got a trade?" Paulo looked at me hopefully, pleased with himself for having made a concrete suggestion.

"The fiancé's a florist by trade. I can promise you a rose garden."

"I'll have a word with the boss," Jean-Charles said. He had the right idea, Monsieur Rosen knew so many people. For the moment, though, there was nothing very inspiring on the horizon. Just problems of space, money, work and work schedules. Why could an Englishman in a posh London club hold up a watch and challenge his fellow club-members, then do a circumnavigation of the globe by balloon and on elephant-back, while François Galarneau, alias The King, even with the help of his friends, could only manage a return trip in a cramped economy-class seat on Air Canada? There was no justice, not even the poetic kind. I knew no generous maharaja living in a lonely palace on the peak of Mount Vindhy and I'd brought back no sad-eyed orphan girls with pockets stuffed with Christmas sparklers to brighten my nights. In the land of pots to wash, beds to make, ham to slice and homework to hand in, the logic of novels was looking nonsensical. Phileas Fogg's salvation was his confidence in things modern. That's the way I should be thinking too. Did Don Quixote take an American Express card on his adventures? Did Gulliver travel by charter? The stories Maman used to read to us in bed, often till dawn, brought visions of Destiny's mighty steed, never of grocery lists.

Our arrival on Fabre Street didn't go unnoticed. Jean-Charles in his car, and Olivier in his, leaned on their horns like Greeks at weddings and all that was missing was the streamers and pink confetti. Nobody was going to start crying again.

31. After unpacking the children's bags, Catherine came to my kitchen. I'd established the tribe in the living-dining room, beds by the walls and the middle for common room,

then the kitchen and my small bedroom. As I opened the cupboards I did what they do at the museum, I gave short historical spiels. Grandmother's earthenware, Maman's blue plates, the everyday dishes. Finally the bathroom. "Isn't there a bidet?" she asked. I blushed, she'd embarrassed me. She should have known that we live in a country conquered by the English, who are particularly strait-laced. Since the Treaty of Versailles we've been washing our feet in the sink and our backsides however we can. It's called Quebec gymnastics.

Monsieur Rosen phoned Dominico's for half a dozen pizzas, all dressed. "*Pizzas tout habillées*" is what he asked for; it's always a literal translation he uses when he can't find either the right words in French or Jean-Charles to help him. The guys had already stocked up on beer and I sent Tatsuro out to get Coke for the children. "That's what everybody drinks in Paris nowadays," I informed him.

There was nothing but baseball on TV, that's the way it is some nights. I explained the rules of the game to the newcomers and made sure the boys knew that from now on, lousy or not, the Expos were going to be their favourite club. You don't nitpick when it comes to pride. What's great about baseball is that the strategy gives you plenty of time to see what's going on. The children caught on faster than Istvan, who persisted in comparing the pitches with shots at goal in soccer. "No, Joachim, the guy's not chewing gum, he chaws tobacco and spits so he'll look like a real man. That's the way it is." But I didn't hide it from anyone that all the Montreal players were Americans and Cubans who got paid a bundle to represent us on the field. "Then they spend the winter in Florida." To the last crumb, they take the cake!

While we waited for the pizza, I went and unpacked my stuff. I'd bought Jean-Charles a book, an early edition of an Alexandre Dumas novel, bound in beautiful red-brown leather, tooled with flowers, three ribs on the spine. It was *Le Comte de Monte Cristo*, I knew he'd already read *Les Trois Mousquetaires* and *Vingt Ans après*. As he thanked me he ran his finger over the gold-leafed title, then smelled the pages. "It smells of last century," he said. Then he put the book to his good ear. "I can hear the horses' hoofs on the cobblestones and the barges passing." After dinner, he took it to a corner and flopped into a chair with his glasses crooked on his nose. My browsing hadn't been in vain.

I offered Monsieur Rosen a stein to drink his beer from, it had belonged to Papa, a wedding present from my grandfather, Aldéric, but he refused politely. He wanted to drink from the bottle to be like the rest of us. "When I was a young man, I used to work pretty hard pushing carts of furs from one factory to another, up and down Bleury Street in mid July. *On n'avait pas de chope à la shop*, so no stein for mine!" I laughed. We have to encourage immigrants to master our language if we want them to integrate. He continued, "I was talking to Catherine in the car on the way here, and she told me Istvan's looking for work. I'll ask Jean-Charles to put him in training. Catherine spoke very highly of you, too. You're very generous."

"Monsieur Rosen, you're the one who's ..."

He cut me off at the pass. "It's occurred to me it would be good to show the family a bit of the country, don't you agree?"

"I was thinking of doing a bus tour of the city, and the Métro goes to Île Sainte-Hélène."

"I mean farther than that. Highways and byways. Quebec City. Chibougamou. You can keep the van, we don't need it right now. You can take till Monday off, we'll get along without you. No problem, we'll figure the cost, it'll just mean a few extra hours. How about it? First impressions are important."

Monsieur Rosen's an old Québécois. He was Joachim's

age when he came to Montreal. It must have been that that got to him. I talked to Catherine and the children about the idea and they clapped their hands for joy.

It was a great party, although six hours of jet lag had us travellers yawning fit to unhinge our jaws. In fact, with people sitting round on the floor, and the beer, the baggage and the smell of pizza, you'd have thought you were at a successful housewarming.

32. I knew I was back in North America as soon as I opened the paper the next morning. On page three was a picture of an ambulance attendant pushing a blood-soaked stretcher. You could imagine the face under the sheet. It belonged to a murdered security guard. He wasn't one of Monsieur Rosen's employees, but still, it gave me an ache in the pit of my stomach. Back to reality.

(CP) A security guard employed by the Secur Company was killed and another wounded yesterday morning during an armed robbery committed by three thugs at the Garland Mall in suburban Montreal.

At least one of the guards is said to have responded by firing at the thieves as they escaped through the parking garage. The bandits were armed with military-type semi-automatic rifles. Five bullet holes were found by police in the garage door. The two guards had been attacked from behind as they were wheeling a hand truck toward their armoured car.

A clerk on duty in a nearby electronics store reported that he thought a film crew must be shooting a sequence on location. There were no screams from any mall customers, only terrified howls from animals in a pet shop.

Of course, there aren't any TVs in pet shops yet to bring the poodles and parrots round, teach them there's no distance any more between make-believe and real life. But when the Secur guard fell to the mall's cold terrazzo floor there was no pause for a message from the sponsor. The gangsters didn't interrupt the program. The mall didn't close its doors. The cash registers kept ringing.

33. I hosed off the van and we left on the wedding trip, Joachim sitting between Maude and me and the other two tads on the rear seat. Catherine and her fiancé stayed at my apartment, only too glad to be alone together at last.

No way were we going to Niagara Falls. Nor was I going to try and sell the others on the Jean Lesage Autoroute with its tumble-down barns and cute little houses. There were still patches of snow scattered here and there in the cornfields, so I told the kids about maple sap, the cold spring nights that keep it running and the smell of it boiling in steam-filled sugarhouses. What they wanted to know was the latest about Michael Jackson and whether we were going to stop at that MacDo up ahead.

"This isn't Hollywood you know, it's Drummondville."

On Cape Diamond in Quebec City they came round. "It feels like home here, it's cool!" I'd pulled tuques down over their heads so all you could see was their almond eyes. Their chatter of curiosity was as constant as a turning prayerwheel. Emerging from the door to the funicular railway on Dufferin Terrace, they agreed that the St. Lawrence River was worth the trip all by itself.

"It's the people I like," said Joachim as he ate his first *poutine*, "I really like the people, they're *sympa*." Eric and Maude began calling me "Papa" when they saw the reaction it got from the Québécois. "Are they boat people?" "Have you adopted them?" I was ringmaster of a helluva circus.

Since there weren't any cowboys, they wanted to see some Indians. I insisted they should see them in their natural state, beside a river, fishing the salmon that were swimming upstream to spawn. But we drove far too long, it was still cold, the highway kept going and going, the children were dead tired and in the twilight all they could see was huts and poor people smoking beside canoes upturned on trestles to dry.

At midnight we were on the foredeck of the ferry to Rivière-du-Loup, near the captain's cabin, huddling together against the wind, between sea and sky, swallowed by the starry night. I had meant to talk to them during the passage about how brave my ancestors had been when they sailed up the St. Lawrence, crossed the Great Lakes, explored the Mississippi, but you can't give your ancestors to people who already have their own, whose grandfathers have paddled on other rivers than yours. I began to realize a lot of things, that their memories stopped at me, so to them *I* was the ancestor, and it was only *my* memory that reached back to Jacques Cartier, Champlain and the Cavelier de La Salle. And when I talked enthusiastically about Percé Rock in the Gaspé, Maude said, "We've seen lots of rocks with holes like that, by the sea in the Algarve." The heritage booster in me was shaken. Monsieur Rosen had goofed.

"D'you know Portugal, François?" I pointed toward the mouth of the St. Lawrence and said, "It's that way." We slept at the well-named Universal Motel.

Since the van had no radio, we made our own music. I hummed my folk ditties, they replied with Roch Voisine; he'd swept Maude and Marianne off their feet when they had been to his fall concert at the Parc des Princes in Paris. At Matane, the clincher came when I tried to teach them to fish smelts from the wharf, and I was the only one to get my fingers dirty and frozen. Éric was surprised the fish were so tiny in so much water. It was time to go home.

I bought them souvenirs on the way back. A headband like the one Arthur wore, a pair of snowshoes, a necklace. Joachim decided on a bow. I promised I'd make him some arrows when we got home.

There wasn't a scratch or a scrape on the van when I gave it back. My head was still full of blue horizons, the cries of gulls and the smell of seaweed clinging to my shoes. The children were enchanted to be back in the city among the skyscrapers and neon signs. Even for the littlest, motorbikes were more exciting than landscapes.

"It's great here, François. Okay, so we learned a lot about corn and maple trees and tobacco and the forest, but we didn't come here to be lumberjacks!"

I got the message. That very evening I took the eldest to the Arcades on Mount Royal Street. It cost me an arm and a leg, but after that he knew it's a civilized country we live in. Still, Nintendo will go the way of Esperanto.

34. When I was back in my uniform and place, in harness at the Garland Mall, anxiety set in. I was more alone now than I had ever been; the excitement of the past few weeks, the plane trip to Europe, Arthur's trial, the phony marriage, the tour with the children and the squatters in my apartment had hidden the truth of the matter. I had found Arthur then lost him again; Jacques had buried himself in his work; Catherine would never replace Marise or Véronique or the loves of my dreams. I guarded my room as a dog does his territory, but nothing else in the apartment was mine any more. Sitting before the monitors in the Mall surveillance booth, I couldn't even rediscover the pleasure I used to find in reading. Jean-Charles had brought me the complete works of Romain Gary, but the books stayed stacked in their pile. Mute. Or perhaps I'd gone deaf.

I did keep looking at the little card a policeman had given me on the train from Brussels to Paris. So far it hadn't been very useful.

We had been sitting in a compartment and Jacques had raised the folding table to hold our coffee and croissants and four mandarin oranges. Two men opened the sliding door, "May we?" Then they sat down across from us and showed their identity cards: Europol. They wanted to check our passports. "The picture doesn't do me justice," I said as I handed them mine. Jacques gave me an exasperated glance.

"Where do you live?"

"Paris temporarily, Montreal usually," Jacques told them.

"Me too," I said, "same as him, but I'm just visiting, it's the first time for me."

"You came to see Nadja Astac yesterday."

"Yes, but we were out of luck," I said and added, "he's as slippery as an eel, you know." I didn't want to look dumb,

84

just innocent.

Jacques was more straightforward. "Look, Arthur has been playing Micmac for fifteen years. We'd lost track of him." He extracted the newspaper cutting from his pocket. "We happened to see his picture and wanted to surprise him."

"And what were you planning to do?"

"I don't know, offer to help perhaps. Arthur may be an oddball but he's no criminal."

"And how do you know that?"

Jacques shrugged.

I said, "He's a Galarneau. He's our brother." They had no right to cast aspersions on a Galarneau, I thought. They continued looking through our passports. I knew the technique, I used it myself sometimes with ruffians. They weren't impressing me that way.

"Your brother's covered a lot of ground since you lost track of him. Were you at the criminal enquiry in Brussels? That was just a pretext so we could hold him. We believe his life is in danger."

How were we to know the story they told us next hadn't been made up? They said that six months earlier Arthur had received a large sum of money from an African country to negotiate an arms purchase. He was supposed to get an approved destination certificate and arrange the shipping. Europol had no proof of anything, but there were a lot of pieces of information that fit together. It could have been a monumental fraud. Six months had passed; Arthur had not made a single arms purchase but had been spending the advance money like water in major hotels. The police in Tripoli were after him, either for themselves or by agreement. Perhaps they had helped him escape. "The better to eliminate him."

A cold chill ran up my spine. It was quite a step from

playing Tintin and the Indian chiefs to arms trafficking. Maybe the headband I had in my suitcase was really Arthur's scalp.

"We're certain your brother will be in touch with you."

Jacques looked at me. He was asking, What are we going to say? What are we going to do?

"He's a master of deceit you know, and we're counting on you to help us." The officers left us their cards, with various telephone numbers and the name of a colleague in Montreal, since I was going home soon.

When they had gone I said to Jacques, "D'you think Arthur might be on the train?"

Jacques shrugged because he's got no imagination. I said to myself, If Arthur's on the *North Star* travelling over the plain at a hundred and twenty kilometres an hour, it's like Agatha Christie. He's as extraordinary as Fregoli, the king of transvestites, I thought. Since then I've been seeing Arthur everywhere, even under my bed.

35. Whenever I passed the Bridal Boutique one floor up in the Mall, which I did several times a day, I wondered what Catherine would have looked like at twenty in one of those dresses with ribbons and tulle at the hips and beads on the bodice. I imagined her in different settings; Arthur wasn't the only one who could play with costumes. She was sexy and always cheerful and smiling, but Istvan kept his eye on her.

With its four incense sticks around it, the Buddha from Villejuif occupied a place of honour on top of my bookcase.

Paulo came to see us every day. It was like a perpetual party in my apartment but I didn't feel like one of the guests. We'd agreed that the tribe would rent an apartment of their own as soon as Istvan had found a job, when there'd been time to let the dust settle and register the children for school.

You can try so hard to please you get to feel like a squeezed lemon. You can try so hard to fit in you get boxed in. Arthur was smarter and Jacques wiser than me. Pleasing Papa, pleasing Maman, pleasing the teacher, pleasing Harry Rosen; I was beginning to suffocate in my uniform.

Things got so bad that that handsome fellow Istvan turned up at the Garland Mall one fine noontime wearing a ridiculous, oversize uniform that made him look like a gigolo on vacation. Monsieur Rosen was sending him to me as an assistant because he hadn't been able to place him anywhere else.

"I did what I could," Jean-Charles said, lifting his hands to the sky. "He's pigheaded, stinks of cologne and won't give up his cheap cigarillos. Apart from that, there aren't any flies on him, believe me. He makes me think of that guy who went with Phileas Fogg, canny and clever. What was his name?"

"Passe-Partout."

That's it, Shyster Partout. You know, at the watchmaker's where I was training him I caught him filling his pockets with watches. To get him off I strung the owner a line that it was an exercise, that if we're going to catch crooks we have to know how to shoplift. That was the part he did best!"

"Did you tell Monsieur Harry about it?"

"No point. You're the boss here. Besides, you know this turkey better than I do. I leave him to you. How's life with the tribe?"

"Come and play cards Saturday night and find out." I needed something to buck me up, it was time for a little blackjack.

While we were talking, Istvan sauntered over to the information counter with his hands in his pockets and began making time with the blonde behind it. Crook or Casanova? I assigned him to the garage. I might have been more cautious. Garland Mall is a huge place and I soon lost sight of him. That very night he ended up in Saint-Luc Hospital, flat on his back like a mummy. Jean-Charles was worried about the agency's reputation and took us all—Catherine, the children and me—to the injured man's bedside.

We hadn't brought any oranges or roses or chocolates. To me he was beginning to look like a rat. When we came into the room, even before saying hello, I took down the torn, dirty uniform that was hanging in the cupboard and wrapped and tied it up like a ham.

"Harry Sécurité trusted you," I said to him. "You can get dressed in something else."

"But what?" he whined. "I haven't got another set of threads!"

Joachim felt his cast and said, "Did you go over Niagara Falls, Istvan?" What he'd gone over was the parapet on Metropolitan Boulevard with a prize Harley-Davidson he hadn't been able to resist.

"Ah, François, you should have heard her purr, like a nice warm broad between my thighs when I mounted her. Her owner had left his helmet hanging on the handle bar, it was as good as inviting me to heist her."

"But you were a security guard! In charge of the parked vehicles! The bike's owner had trusted it to you personally!"

"Trusted it to *me*?"

Istvan had full-throttled out of there, didn't know his way around the city and found himself on the Laurentian Autoroute beyond Sainte-Adèle. He was coming back when an overload rig passed him going like a bullet. Crowded and startled, he swerved suddenly, lost control and fell twenty feet.

"At least ten metres!" he wailed.

"He's a liar besides," Jean-Charles growled in my ear.

Like Istvan, the bike had come out of it mangled, not even in condition to stand when propped.

Months of physio in view. In the next bed, behind a half-drawn cotton curtain, an old man was muttering fretfully. Catherine went to comfort him and pull his covers over his shoulders. The fiancé realized he was inspiring less sympathy than his neighbour.

"*Merde!* Didn't you bring any cigarillos?"

"You expected us to bake you a cake too?" Jean-Charles replied, fuming. "It's Harry Sécurité that's going to foot the bill, and maybe we'll get sued besides, so you've stopped smoking." Then he led the rest of us to the elevator.

36. Joachim didn't forget my promise. He badgered me till we went to the mountain and cut some sticks and I turned them into small, sharp arrows. He went to bed all excited and had hardly slept at all when I came to wake him before Galarneau showed his nose the next morning. The dawn was candy pink when we set off on tiptoe along the neighbourhood lanes. Hunting is a state of grace, it awakens the senses; the tiniest sound becomes a trail to be followed. I'd promised him not a moose but rabbits and squirrels.

Holding his bow at the ready with an arrow drawn, Joachim went ahead and I followed three paces behind, camera in hand so I could immortalize his takes. We spotted an animal moving in the shadows of a yard; it was as big as a lion and as fast as a leopard and knocked over garbage cans with crashing sounds. Joachim shot his arrow and missed. The raccoon climbed a tree and looked down on us as though we'd stepped out of a Hemingway novel.

"What are we going to do, François?"

"I can get a picture of him, but I don't think he'll come down for the rest of the day."

On the way home across the vacant lot at the corner of the boulevard, Joachim came face to face with a skunk. I yelled, "No, no, don't shoot!" but the fearless hunter ran around behind the mass of black and white fur gallumping toward shelter. And got what he deserved. I mean to say, the natives have a right to defend themselves against immigrants who don't respect their territory. That's what I told Catherine when I asked her to go and buy several cans of tomato juice to bathe her son in because he stank of skunk at twenty feet. I took a photo of him looking miserable and nearly in tears, and explained that this would be proof he'd slain the dragon and so wasn't a child any more. Although the stench was so bad it was all I could do not to make a face, I was convinced that this would be one of the best mornings of his life.

"Did you get it from a skunk when you were little?"

"I got worse. Three beavers upset my canoe and dumped me in ice-cold water. I couldn't swim." I made it up as I went along and Joachim began to laugh.

In the days when Arthur, Jacques and I were setting traps in the underbrush, nobody had taken photos of our hunts. At least, how could any of us know? In a frenzy of cleaning up, Maman had thrown the family photo album in the garbage because she couldn't recognize anyone in the pictures any more. When you've lost your memory, the faces you once glued lovingly on those black pages turn into snaps that hurt.

37. Even stuck in a hospital bed, being out of circulation was something Istvan didn't accept gracefully. He would have broken out of his cast and come to defend his interests if he'd known I wasn't indifferent to Catherine.

He was an enterprising fellow; two weeks after arriving on Saint-Luc Hospital's fourth floor, with the help of a male nurse he had control of cigarette sales. His condition was improving by leaps and bounds. He bought himself satin sheets, flowered pillows and a bottle of whiskey; with *Playboy* and *Paris-Match*, his standard equipment was complete.

He became a devotee of cable television, a remote-control changer never far from hand. Thus he became a faithful viewer of the programme *Well Done, Neighbour!*, a variety show which purported to demonstrate that truth is stranger than fiction. Anyone suggesting a candidate neighbour who was subsequently featured on the programme received a thousand dollars and a chance in the monthly draw for a Cadillac Eldorado. The neighbour had to be a noteworthy person who had accomplished something exceptional. There had been a lady bush pilot, a heroic fireman, Henry Ford's grandson and a workingman priest who performed miracles. Istvan hastened to cash in by fingering his own neighbour, a man he sincerely admired, who had given himself so that a brother and sister, separated by war, could be reunited. The producers liked the suggestion. I wouldn't go along. When Monsieur Rosen heard about it he insisted I appear, and in uniform. An hour on television could be useful to Harry Sécurité.

A television camera crew came to the Garland Mall and taped me from all angles. They had me strike poses and catch a pickpocket who was really just the cameraman's assistant. I felt like an idiot, all at sixes and sevens. On Tuesday evening three days later, Catherine, the four children and I were on the set at the television station. We'd been powdered, made up, coiffed and warned, "Just reply briefly to the host's questions, the visuals will speak for themselves." Paulo was waiting in the wings for the grand finale, the sibling reunion. I wasn't displeased to see Joachim with eyes so wide they were almost round, watching the technical deployment; perhaps he might choose a trade in television some day.

Music borrowed from Big Bazar opened the program. There was pathos over the plight of refugees, views of pre-revolution Cambodian landscapes and cities, then demonstrations and murders in progress, and those thousands of skulls of Pol Pot's victims, sun-bleached, heaped up like pyramids raised to commemorate horror. We didn't know that during this time the cameras were trained on us, recording our revulsion and the hysterical tears shaking Catherine.

"That's good, that's very good!" a floor director murmured into his headset mini-mike. "Keep it up, Madame!"

I couldn't just sit there, I ran to Catherine and took her in my arms. "It's over, don't cry any more, there, there!" And into her ear I whispered, "You're here now, in Quebec, you're safe." The program host came forward, the children clustered around us, and I said to the popinjay, "What you're doing is cruel! The children have never known war. Their mother had put it out of her mind. Why d'you want to wake up these ghosts?"

"And did *you* know these things, Monsieur Galarneau?"

"It's *because* I knew them that I agreed to go to Paris and marry Catherine, so she could rejoin her brother, so she could forget the horror."

That was exactly what they'd wanted me to say, because straight off they showed the tape they'd taken at the Garland Mall. I looked pretty good but you couldn't see the Harry Sécurité crest very well, so Monsieur Rosen was going to be disappointed. While I walked past the stores, watched the surveillance monitors or chased the designated pickpocket, the host read a grandiloquent text in a full, rich voice, evoking a security guard's generosity, spirit of sacrifice, open-heartedness, desire to share the planet, amen. Then it was time for Paulo, followed by a spotlight, to go and join his sister, who was smiling again now.

Maude, Eric and Mariannne stayed sitting with straight backs on their stools, but Joachim began to fidgit. He came and tugged at my sleeve. "Say, François, can we go? What are we here for?"

"So Istvan can put a thousand dollars in his pocket."

"I want to go!"

"Soon, Joachim, soon." But he escaped from me and ran crying to his mother because he was afraid, not understanding what was going on. The cameras lapped it up and surrounded us with light and music. *Well Done, Neighbour!* had scored again.

For two whole weeks people were congratulating me on the sidewalk, on the Métro, on the job, and I even signed autographs. Harry Sécurité had been mentioned in the credits and got contracts from the government; the Minister of Immigration had been touched by the story. Then everything calmed down and I returned to my books and my crusades. Jean-Charles recommended a second-hand book he had found, *Voyage au bout de la nuit*. When day broke I slipped the Europol card between its leaves. Arthur had become my book marker.

38. Perhaps one day I was going to be immortalized by someone putting a plaque on the house on Île Perrot: "In this house was born François Galarneau, primitive writer and author of his own misfortunes."

We were barely into June when an unusually hot and humid spell descended on the city. One morning, with the window closed and a silent fan trained on my pillow, I lay asleep as still as a stone on a cool river bed. I was sweating, wondering whether I was dreaming. I perceived sweetness and movement between my sheets this morning, finger tips caressing me, then what I recognized as lips against my navel, a nose brushing gently from side to side. I was now wide awake with a hard-on like a fence post. Softly as a partridge, Catherine had slipped into my bed.

"We're married, François." Her tone was half solemn, half cajoling. She snuggled up to me. "And I've decided to leave Istvan." Her warmth reached me hotter than the heat of June through her silk nightshirt.

"It's Istvan who left us, isn't it?" I said.

I propped myself on a hip and looked into her eyes. They were like dark, soft chestnuts behind the slits. Somehow, surely by association, I thought of a conversation I'd had with Jacques one night when he took me to see the Champs Élysées.

I'd observed girls with nicely turned posteriors, skirts asshole length, black bags slung across a shoulder. Expensive cars would slow down, the girls would bend to the windows, breastworks to the fore. Shopping, prices negotiable. Jacques explained that the air in the City of Light was aphrodisiac. Style and beauty.

"In Paris, writers associate writing with sexuality, you know. Having writer's block, they always say, is like not being able to get it up, see? And vice versa."

"Do you get it up these days?" I detected discomfiture in his face.

"Not every day. Victor Hugo used to say he had a bone in his pants." After all these years, Jacques was still on his first manuscript.

We walked up the avenue on the odd-number side and came back on the sidewalk opposite. It was warm and pleasant. Around us, people were speaking all the tongues of the planet. I liked these colourful, cosmopolitan crowds, these Japanese in western garb, theatrical Italians, tall Americans in jogging suits, but Jacques pursued his line of thought, "When a woman writes, I wonder if she thinks about the erection of her clitoris."

"You're a bit of a dork at times, Jacques!" I said this with a laugh because I could see him shriveling up the way a mushroom wilts, gnawed at by a brain that never stopped cogitating.

In Cambodia, Pol Pot would have bumped him off with a single shot, I read this in Catherine's eyes that were as dark as the waters of a pond.

She was holding me closer and closer. "Catherine, it's not that I don't want to." I was making a fool of myself, she could feel with her hand that I was losing it by the second. Only penises don't lie, Arthur used to say when he stepped on the dance floor.

She didn't insist. "Shall I make us some tea?" She stroked my cheek and then got up.

I stayed in the kitchen a long time, sipping the steaming hot infusion, standing at the window where I could watch the sun heating the grey back sheds. I remembered the last thing Jacques had said that night as we walked down the stairs of the Franklin D. Roosevelt Station. A smell of burning rubber was rising from the Métro tunnels. I'd asked him if there was a woman in his life in Paris. He looked at me, the glare of the station's yellow lights on his face.

"There are lots of them in my book!" he replied.

39. Why do I love literature so, I often wonder. What does it do for me? It would be easier to slip video cassettes in a VCR and let myself be entertained in colour and costume. But I keep coming back to the bookshelves. To me, literature, from Persian prayers all the way to newsstand pulp, is truly humanity thinking out loud.

If one of the literary magazines asked my opinion, this is what I'd say. But journalists don't have time for a relay race that's been going on for centuries. They have to discover the ultimate work the world has been waiting for, it's novelty they're after. I'm just trying to slip in among the pack. I imagine us writers to be like the countless runners who turn out wearing numbered bibs for a marathon every year; now and then one of us breaks out ahead and the one trailing the pack gives up, but the human tide that sets off is us and the race has been going on ever since scribes appeared along with writing.

I'm not sure what number I've been given to wear, I just know I've trained for this marathon; I don't want to win, I just want to be part of it, and anyway my running shorts are all threadbare and my finish-line photo wouldn't be usable because I'd raise my right arm, fist clenched, and people would see holes in my singlet.

40. "Hello! Am I speaking to Eric's father?"

Eric's father was the doorman at the George V in a ritzy part of Paris, but I said, "What can I do for you?"

"I'm the school principal. I'd urgently like to see you. Can you come to my office early this afternoon?"

"What's up?"

Has the kid gone and snitched a motor bike? I wondered.

"I'll expect you at two o'clock, Monsieur Galarneau."

The principal, Monsieur Desautel, was a man of my own age with an advanced case of baldness and huge, bushy white eyebrows. He looked like a successful cross between a billiard ball and a worn broom. To assert his authority, looking like that, he must have had to play drill sergeant with the children. I kept imagining nicknames he must have been graced with while he told me how he went about detecting *manifestations of delinquency*. He pronounced the expression as if he were sucking on a jujube.

Eric arrived with his head down and a mulish look on his face.

I asked, "Is he a bad student?"

"No, quite the contrary. First in Math, top of the class in French."

"What then?"

Monsieur Desautel opened the drawer of his desk, took out an envelope and handed it to me. "Count this."

I did. I counted nearly six hundred dollars. Then I closed my eyes and took a deep breath, as Salem had taught me to do. Time to calm the sea. I'd read so much about goings-on in suburban Paris. I looked Catherine's son in the eye.

"You're working for Istvan?"

"No way."

"You're pushing?"

97

"You haven't got the picture," Monsieur Desautels said. "He sells home-made lottery tickets, using this to convince reluctant buyers." The principal tossed a knife on the table; it was sharp enough to dispatch an ox. "A dollar a ticket, fifty for the prize. He makes the draw himself. As he puts it "*Ça boume*, it's a hit.""

"Gambling's not allowed in Canada? Wouldn't have come if I'd known."

Monsieur Desautels was not fond of either policemen or journalists and was sure that Monsieur Galarneau would know what to do with a delinquent. A Harry Sécurité agent, he thought, should have more than one technique in his bag of tricks.

Eric and I went home without exchanging a word. At an age when I hadn't yet taken my first communion, Eric was going to have to be exorcised.

41. The court sat in the dining room. I had put on my best blue uniform, my polished shoes, my blue shirt. Joachim was beside me with a plastic revolver in his belt, representing the State. Jean-Charles was acting as judge. In his right hand he held a wooden mallet which he used both for cracking walnuts and calling for silence. On his head, for a judge's wig, he had put a beaten-up floor mop. I begged him to remove it.

The jury was ensconced on two rows of chairs: Catherine, as anxious as if she were attending a voodoo ceremony, Paulo, chewing his nails, and the two girls, Marianne, who was as tense as her mother, and Maude, who would rather have been watching television. Eric was slouched in his seat with an ashtray on his lap. The telephone was on its stool with the receiver off the hook so the fiancé could hear everything from his hospital bed.

"Defendant, rise and state your family name, given name and role in society." Jean-Charles had just smashed the plate instead of the walnut he had meant to crack. While the jury tittered, I rose and replied anyway.

"It is precisely my role in society that is in question, your honour."

Jean-Charles was enjoying himself, not understanding that this trial was in fact serious because my life had become a parody.

"What charge are you bringing against yourself?" This was in the true tradition of the Inquisition, with the priest in the confessional making us recite our turpitudes and beg absolution.

"I'm charging myself with being an incompetent intermediary. As a delegate of a Quebec Committee for the Reconciliation of Families, I agreed first of all to be an accessary to an impersonation. My guilt is the worse for the fact that I had no confidence whatever in the devious individual who moreover was my wife's lover."

"Monsieur Galarneau, I am interrupting you for a minute," Jean-Charles said, succeeding this time in breaking the nut he was aiming at. "Have you derived therefrom any personal benefit in the form of salary, emoluments or inadmissable satisfactions?"

The nuts were giving me a thirst for justice. "Go get me a beer," I said to Joachim. The sheriff hastened to the refrigerator.

"That is for you to decide," I said to the judge. "I moved Dame Catherine, her children and her fiancé in with my furniture, undertook a peregrination in my boss's vehicle with the youngest to acquaint them with our Quebec mode of life and agreed to have Madame's lover wear the uniform of the Earth and Lightening Bolt, thus facilitating the immigrant's initial step in assuming his economic role."

"I am aware of this," the judge said, "It was even I who initiated the action."

Both of us enjoyed using vocabulary gleaned from our readings. The best compliment you could pay Jean-Charles was to tell him, "You talk like a great book." Then he would become expansive, glow with confidence, as if literature protected him from human malice.

Joachim handed me a beer which he'd opened himself. Maude had fallen asleep sucking her thumb.

All of us have some mannerism, something deeply ingrained, a tic or minor gesture, pulling an earlobe, scratching one's nose, clearing one's throat involuntarily, that surfaces when we're prey to emotion. I stroked my eyelids with my left index finger; Maman used to put us to sleep this way. I said, "And then I trusted Istvan, and he betrayed me. That was my second error."

Jean-Charles seized the telephone receiver from the stool. "You hear that, Istvan? What have you got to say about that?" He listened attentively to the injured man at the other end. The rest of us kept silent meanwhile. Then he put the receiver down, gently so as not to jar the ear of the fiancé, who was already in such fragile condition.

"Istvan says that the facts are correct, but he is deeply wounded to learn that you did not bear him the same high regard that he bore for you. If you did not like him, you should not have proceeded. He adds that one evening in the course of his floral rounds he took you on a tour of Paris and bought you drinks at every stop. He considers that a man who's got bum-balls, excuse me ladies but it's Istvan talking, ought not to go drinking with someone he despises, distrusts or does not consider his friend. He goes on to say that you shamelessly imbibed so many glasses of champagne that when he took you home you climbed the stairs to your brother's on your hands and knees. He can get corroboration from two garbagemen who helped him drag you from the car to the stairs. He still remembers that you were singing *La Marseillaise*, not realizing that he, the Hungarian, and the two garbagemen, a big black West Indian and a *petit-beurre* ..." Jean-Charles broke off, his mallet poised in the air. "Catherine, *petit-beurre*, that's a biscuit?"

"It's the son of a *harki*, an Algerian born in France. It means 'Arab' in the code-slang called 'Verlan'. B. e. u. r., 'beur'."

"Oh. Whatever. Istvan adds that all three of them were more French than you, a two-bit Canadian, and your singing was in poor taste."

It's true I'd had a blast that night.

"Istvan adds further that if somebody pays his return fare he'll go and find the two witnesses in Paris. What do you say?"

I was speechless. What twisted hogwash! Istvan would park on the sidewalk, usually in front of a small bistro, the children would go off with baskets of roses on their arms and we'd wait for them at the bar, where he'd introduce me to the owner ("a Canadian friend," he'd say) and sometimes some regulars, who'd drink with us. I didn't get the hang of all they were saying about well-stacked bimbos, hey-hey, who'd give them pipe jobs, hee-hee! I know they knew all there was to know about sports, loved poodles and voted communist.

"I admit I went overboard," I replied, "I really tied one on, but now I'm sober and I'd like to know if Istvan is aware what a bad influence he has been. Does he know that Eric has been practicing extortion at school?"

There was a crackling on the telephone. Jean-Charles

took the receiver.

"Our biker says he had nothing to do with that."

Then Paulo stood up, spat out a last piece of fingernail and launched into an incoherent babble, a mishmash about his hopes of paying his debts, races at Blue Bonnets, and his nephew, who had been trying to help him.

"I'm his godfather. He's a good boy. He has to be excused."

Jean-Charles began cracking nuts.

I said, "There's going to be a Galarneau eclipse, I think. Your lordship will be good enough to condemn Paulo to take responsibility for the tribe, he's the silent partner, after all. I'm throwing in my cards."

Joachim looked at me, puzzled. "To the last crumb," I said to him, "and they're not even Americans."

His lordship drove me to work. At last I knew what made the Buddha smile.

42. Three months later, the tribe was still living in my apartment. I hardly ever set foot there myself. I'd set up a bed in a cubby-hole at Garland, ate out and went to movies in the afternoon. I even stopped picking my movie, for its category or actors, I mean. I wanted a comfortable seat, a wide screen, stereo sound and salty popcorn. Movies aren't life, they're entertainment. I was being entertained.

Istvan had gone back to Paris on crutches. I'd driven him to Mirabel Airport with relief. Now I was square with the authorities. Paulo and Catherine were thinking of opening a restaurant and had taken steps to have their aged mother join them. It wasn't an expression of filial piety; they wanted to put her to work in the kitchen because none of the children knew anything about Cambodian cooking. In the eyes of immigration officials, family reunification no doubt has a cultural dimension.

I'd contacted the RCMP several times at the number the Europol gumshoe had given me. Information-providing ought to be a two-way street. It still wasn't known where Arthur had got to, or what name he was using. The only new slant on the case was a report from Amsterdam. Under the name Pierre Saint-Hilaire, my brother had founded the World University, a non-profit organization which, for a respectable fee, would bestow equivalences on individuals whose university degrees were short on prestige. Armed with a certificate of equivalence, anyone could claim to have as good as a doctorate from Yale, the Sorbonne or Oxford. I wrote for one myself; I wouldn't have spat on a degree, but it was mostly so I'd get a letter from Arthur. The policeman had told me I'd be wasting my time. The envelope came all the way back from Holland because the World University had closed its doors four years before. Policemen are right sometimes.

Once in a while I stopped in at Fabre Street. It was like paying myself a visit, inquiring what was new with me, picking up my mail. Each time, Catherine insisted I stay for lunch and Joachim gave me a chess lesson. Paulo had moved into my room. "Don't worry, if I borrow one of your books I'll put it back where it belongs." I'd leave with clean clothes and almond cookies, a present from Marianne, who had begun cooking. The children were beginning to take their place in the sun. I kept paying the rent but for the rest the tribe was supposed to manage on its own, which it was doing.

"How long are you going to stay in your catacomb?"

Jean-Charles often asked me. In a miniscule room on the lower street level at the Mall, I'd set up a sofa-bed, desk-table and lamp, all bought in Mall stores. I kept my books in boxes. I was reading Boris Vian and sipping gin sold by the warehouse liquor store next door to my room. Big moonscape posters on the walls made a space ship of the place.

I thought briefly about founding *Guards Without Borders* to help the blue berets here and there in the world. The UN soldiers would disarm the combatants and restore peace, and then we would arrive to keep order. The planet really needed our services, and on all five continents. Arthur would have found a way to put the plan into action. I didn't have the energy any more. Since my one experience in international affairs hadn't panned out, why would I leave the Garland Mall, my castle? Everything I needed was here: books, newspapers, food, drink, entertainment. I was punctual arriving at work and my reports were submitted on time. I really had no desire even to go and play cards at Tatsuro's. So when Jean-Charles transmitted the invitation to dine at Monsieur Rosen's the following Monday, I figured they must be afraid I was losing my marbles.

"Was it you who suggested this to the boss to get me out of here?"

"Never. Do what you like, François, I don't even know what he wants to talk to you about."

43. Monsieur Rosen's house was at the end of a crescent of asphalt between two huge catalpa trees. Miraculous that these trees hadn't frozen to death sometime in the last twenty

years. Even the maples on the street had been winter-damaged, every other branch as bare as a chicken's foot. I was dressed in uniform, had my wedding cap on, and at my left shoulder had added a white cord like the ones worn by security guards at the Louvre. You have to hand it to the French, they've really got style. I was coming reluctantly, like an officer calling on his general the night before a losing battle. I rang the doorbell dutifully, gazing up at the slate roof, which didn't go well with the rose windows.

When the door opened I was struck dumb, turned in a twinkling to a pillar of salt. I'd expected to see Harry Rosen, his potato nose bobbing in a sea of wrinkles, his curly white hair like a halo around his pate. What I saw before me was a model from Gucci's, the pinnacle of elegance whatever the latitude. Then Perfection moved her lips, a radiant smile illuminated the flawless oval of her face, a dimple appeared as if by witchery, her green eyes sparkled and I removed my cap and bowed, as one must always do in the presence of Beauty. Thus I perceived that from head to foot this woman had been blessed by the gods.

"You're Monsieur Galarneau?"

"For sure it's François!" a voice behind her said, and Monsieur Rosen appeared in the doorway, putting his arm around the shoulders of my seraphic vision. "François, this is Helen, my wife."

I'd seen it before, back in Paris, old beaux, rich celebrities, strolling in the evening after dinner on the Boulevard St. Germain, with chicks dedicated to the nation's treasures and thirty years younger on their arms.

I made brave to kiss her hand. Her fingers were long, tapered and warm. Beauty and The Beast bade me enter.

The vestibule was cluttered with copper weather-vanes: cocks, horses, a pig with its tail in the air, ducks in flight, all mounted on vertical stems anchored in polished wood stands. "You start collecting baseball cards and you end your days living in a glory hole." Monsieur Rosen collected everything. Old china, Inuit sculpture, crystal of the kind you find at Henry Birks and Sons, purveyor to kings and queens. There was stuff everywhere, in glass cases, on the walls, under the furniture. "I love rare and beautiful things."

"Madame Rosen's no discredit to your collections," I ventured. The angel, laughing, insisted that I call her Helen. My interest in life was reviving. Helen!

We went and sat in a room that had been designed as the drawing room; it was jammed with Victorian furniture that was too big and heavy for the space, icons vied with station clocks on the walls, there was a clutter of pinwheels behind the sofa, and lightening rods on a low table gave me the illusion of overlooking the rooftops of a village. This house was an encyclopedia!

While Helen poured us each a glass of port—"very old," Monsieur Rosen stressed, "as old as me"—I never took my eyes off her. She moved with the slightest roll of the hips which further rounded her curves. Monsieur Rosen had discovered the secret of paradise: sex with an angel.

"To your health, François!" Helen said, raising her glass above a cock that had once topped a steeple. I had a wild urge to climb up it. "Daddy tells me you're his best employee."

So Harry was called "Daddy" in private. Deserved it, too.

"I'm not sure I understand, Madame."

"What I told her, François, is that you have unusual capacities, that you're a kind of poet in our organization, and that I have total confidence in you."

What were they leading up to? My intellectual capacities had got me where I was. Period. Paragraph. I didn't want either pity or admiration, just a little respect. Were they looking for a partner in a triangle? Had I become the subject of break-fast-table conversation between Helen and Rosen? I did have a lot of trouble squaring my emotions with my thinking, but don't we all? Why did Harry Rosen collect things like a second-hand dealer? So none of it would get away from him. When he lost his memory one day, like Maman, Harry Rosen would go wandering, alone and forlorn, among knick-knacks he wouldn't even be able to put names to any more.

"Your brother's still in Paris?"

"Yes. He's finishing a novel. Arthur's abroad too. I'm the only Galarneau holding the fort." I kept seeing Helen's legs in flashes between two Daum crystal figurines. I felt outside of time and space, dizzied by erotic emanations. Which novel had already shown me this scene? Why had they invited me? I told myself, I'm going to love her in silence, no one's going to know about this feeling that's come over me, it's beyond price anyway.

With rich people, you eat in bits and pieces. Trays and dishes overflowed with smoked fish, olives, hors d'oeuvres, salads and grains, tastefully arranged between two candelabra. Helen invited me to taste this and that. Caviar and vodka. I had my mouth full when Monsieur Rosen came to the point.

"François, I could simply have had you assigned to the job I'm going to talk to you about, but it's a ticklish matter and I wanted to meet you outside the workaday context."

"Daddy, you're beating around the bush!"

I said to myself, If he wants to, let him go ahead and talk three times the clock around, I'm by your side, pretty lady!

"Here we go, then. Helen is to give a talk soon in Philadelphia and then again in New York."

"I teach history of art," the lovely creature said.

Monsieur Rosen had agreed to let his wife take his collection of erotic miniatures with her—superb, tiny pictures as old as Methuselah, painted in India and Persia—but the insurers wanted exorbitant premiums. The exhibition was getting to be out of the question.

"They want two hundred thousand dollars, you might as well know." The collection was worth perhaps ten times that, he didn't know exactly. Would I agree to travel with and look after the works? He offered me a bonus under the table, five thousand dollars paid in advance for eight working days.

"Say yes, François. I absolutely have to give this talk and the exhibition is an indispensable part of it. I'm writing a book on the subject ..."

"Ah, well, if you're writing a book ..."

I had some more vodka, filled up my spoon with this sturgeon jam, which I crushed against my palate before swallowing. Set sail with a crew like this? Jean-Charles himself would be drooling at the chance.

"Good for you!" the woman of my dreams exclaimed. "We leave in three weeks. And my talk and the exhibition will increase the value of your collection, Harry, so you won't lose out, either. That's what history of art's all about."

As I walked home with red cheeks and wobbly legs, Montreal was beginning to bed down for the winter, a smell of burning leaves in the air. I didn't need to think about Helen, she had enveloped me like an evening dew. I shivered as I whistled blues tunes the way Papa liked them, in the dark.

44. The days before leaving passed quickly. At night as I walked the empty spaces of the Garland Mall I imagined the conversations I was going to have with the beautiful Helen.

When the next day came, I never managed to see her alone. She treated me correctly, nothing more, and the subtle emanations I'd felt that first evening had evaporated. I was almost sorry I'd been so quick to accept the job they were offering. I should have left them wanting me. I wanted her, didn't I? In the offices she took me to, I would study her secretly, watching for the slightest sign of complicity, every cell in my body straining toward her.

Bypassing the specialist insurance companies didn't mean Monsieur Rosen could also bypass the complex customs requirements; there were endless forms to fill out, a meticulous description of each work with a Polaroid picture, seals and expert witnesses for authentication. Three afternoons carefully wrapping each of the things in the shipping rooms of the Museum of Fine Arts on Sherbrooke Street. Choosing the frames. Helen behaved in a professional manner in front of the curator and his carpenters. Not a single off-colour joke. I went to her appointments in uniform and, while taking notes so I could direct the hanging of the exhibition, kept a serious face. What I was doing was scrupulously preparing a trip for forty erotic pictures specially chosen to turn the Americans on. To the last crumb, those Americans! Miniatures sent to do a giant's job.

Words are full of surprises. I thought to myself, These miniatures are a good idea, kings who have to cart their worldly goods about on the backs of elephants can't load up with bas-reliefs. Nomads aren't dumb. Then, between one certificate search and the next, Helen told us these works weren't called miniatures because they were small but because they were coated with minium, a pigment obtained by oxidizing molten lead. In the pictures there was nothing miniature about the penises, you'd say they'd been coated with hard-on creams. When I next saw Jean-Charles I told him

109

what awe and admiration I had for them. "I don't know what the Persians before Jesus Christ used to eat, dear fellow, but they had dicks as long as umbrellas and as thick as your arm."

"Must be art," Charlie replied with a straight face, "it can't surely have anything to do with reality. Unless, between Adam and us, evolution has been moving toward smaller models."

"Well, if I'm to believe your theory, Adam must have carried round his equipment in a wheelbarrow! I don't know why the boss collects smutty stuff like that."

"Monsieur Rosen's no saint."

"Have you met his wife?"

"I've seen her on occasion, she's a stunner. I get to drive her round town once in a while. She's just back from Switzerland where her brother lives. Between the two world wars, their mother took care to have each of her three sons born in a different country. They managed to thrive on it. Smart woman, she invested her eggs for the long term."

"D'you think the boss keeps those sexy miniatures to help him get it up? She's not his age."

"Do those acrobatics do it to you?"

"In the state I'm in now, yes."

"Meaning?"

"When I set eyes on Helen Rosen, I'm afraid lightening struck."

"In his house? With all those lightening rods? Couldn't have!"

Jean-Charles didn't want to hear me talk about Helen, perhaps out of loyalty to Monsieur Harry. So as I bit into a sushi I made do with picturing the tip of her breast, the colour of raw salmon.

45. The following Monday I dropped by Fabre Street. The leaves were already beginning to turn yellow and the neighbour, who was always ahead of things, was putting on his double windows.

Joachim was in bed with a fever, as lumpy with pustules as an old tree. He showed me his back and I told him, "It's gorgeous, like a map of the sky showing constellations. You've been blessed by the gods." But he cried because he wasn't allowed to scratch. I told him all about my chickenpox, my mumps, my scarlet fever, my bubonic plague, my yellow fever, my tetanus and cholera. If I'd survived, so would he. Then he felt so good he sat up in bed and drew me magnificent landscapes to put up on the walls of my cubby-hole.

"Better still, I'm going to take your drawings on a trip, along with the boss's pictures. I'll exhibit them in a big gallery in the States and you'll get to be rich and famous."

"Will you come back, François?"

"What d'you think? I'm going on a return trip with the star fairy. When I get back there won't be a single spot left on your tummy." But Joachim didn't want to be rich and famous, all he wanted was to hold my hand. Through the open window we could hear the other children kicking a football in the yard. Paulo was keeping both goals and betting on the results.

Catherine handed me a letter from Jacques which was waiting on the sideboard. My brother was leaving for Moscow on a reporting assignment. Should Canadians invest in these new markets? What had happened to the Russian parliament? Had the Mafia taken over everything? And then a piece on the ecology there. Jacques wasn't displeased with this interruption, he regarded it as an escape to the land of Dostoyevsky. His novel was at a standstill, the chestnut trees of Paris weren't inspiring him any more, maybe birches might change his inner landscape. "Perhaps I'll run into Arthur in Red Square," he added, "and we'll drink a vodka to your health." How could he know that this very liquor, ice-cold, had become my fetish drink since Helen had wet her luscious lips with it? Next I was dreaming of rolling with her in a prairie full of buffalo grass. I sighed.

"Bad news?" Catherine asked. I looked up and we exchanged a smile, and I returned to earth. "I've had a letter from Paris too, you know," she continued. It could only be a letter from the fiancé, risen from the dead.

"Have they nailed Istvan at last?"

Her eyes fell to her apron. "He wants me to marry him." Nothing was going to make this fellow back off.

"Istvan wants to come back *here*?"

"He says he misses Montreal a lot, that there are plenty of opportunities here ..."

"There are plenty of motorbikes, yes." I couldn't believe she still even gave him a thought. But I was in love too, so I could be sympathetic. "You've really got that Hungarian under your skin, haven't you? What would you like us to do?"

"We could get divorced."

I'd overlooked this detail; why not take advantage of it to break away altogether this time? I might even announce the news to Helen and tell her I was doing it for her. If she did likewise we could elope to Bermuda and make love under the palms till we were spent.

"All right," I said, "when I get back we'll arrange it. I'll even look for a wedding present for you in New York. Something hideous and expensive that you won't ever dare get rid of."

"Children! Marianne! François is going to the States, come and say goodbye."

I kissed them and turning to Paulo said, "In Red Square or on Broadway, Galarneau shines for everyone!" I mean, it put sunshine in my heart to be setting off for the States, it reminded me of my truckdriver days and wanting to get away and knowing for sure that one day soon I'd be lost in that cosmopolitan crowd you find in the cities to the South.

Back in the cubby-hole, I phoned the Drinkwater in Boston before going on duty. When you call around five o'clock you know you're going to get your party because in these big institutions they serve dinner before sundown. A question of order and union organization. The head nurse warned me that Maman was becoming neurasthenic and spent her afternoons at the solarium window muttering her name.

"Maman, I wanted to tell you I'm going to be away for a few days and you mustn't try and reach me."

"My poor Arthur, I don't even remember your phone number. My memory does play tricks on me, you know."

"This is François, Maman."

"What are you phoning me for?"

"I wanted to know if Jacques had written you. He's going to Russia for his paper."

"Which Jacques?"

"It doesn't matter. Are you eating well, Maman?"

"I want to go home. I'm lonesome here."

"What are you lonesome for?"

"For life."

I looked at the telephone with its coiled umbilical cord. There's no justice, I said to myself, and they promise us eternity! There's only birth and death, we know that. Maman too had known what it was like to fall in love, and had basked in the pleasures of picking strawberries and lying on the grass in the woods and choosing a different dress to put on and hoping for an encounter. I was following in her footsteps, but who was going to follow in mine?

46. I packed my notebooks between my blue shirts, put my pen in a polished shoe with some rolled-up black socks, and since I didn't intend to go alone I asked Réjean Ducharme, Albert Camus and Philip Roth to go with me. With bozos like that along, I could face any horde and any problem.

With my replacement on the job and the cubby-hole locked up, I went to the airport in a company van while Monsieur Rosen drove with Helen in the limousine. Jean-Charles wore his white gloves. The lady was travelling business class and I was to go in a cargo plane by another route with the erotic crates. I didn't protest. A Harry Sécurité agent, even when escorting works of art, even when a guest at the boss's table, is still just an employee. Your humble servant.

I hadn't seen my angel all week but we'd talked on the telephone, and each time her warm breath had made me glow. Still, it was as plain to see as the Persian kings' peckers that I'd been fantasizing a romance, I wasn't going to be travelling with the one I loved. I was parked on a cargo ramp, where Jean-Charles came and found me. He felt responsible for my unhappiness. "I got you reading too many novels," he told me, "and now you expect life to be the way it is in books. You and she were born to different cradles." He'd taken off his white gloves. I told him to go to hell, that I knew better than he did where to look for real life, the one you want back when your memory's gone, the one you write about to get the better of death, when your Galarneau's all screwed up, your brain full of sunstorms and your body burning out of control. How can a feeling that's so buoyant and pure, that has Chagall fiancés dancing on rooftops, turn into a whop in the ribs?

Jean-Charles stayed standing beside the car; he was to drive Monsieur Rosen home. I saw him through the plane window and we waved. I buckled my seat belt, with an infernal noise the big bird moved off, away from the grey hangar, it sped down the runway, no one could have stopped it, then it rose with a heave and under the vibrating wings I suddenly discovered how beautiful the city was. And I thought, In all things you have to stay high, because on the ground there are always crocodiles with open jaws, hoping to get you.

47. The talk by Mrs. Helen D. Rosen, R.C.A.A., entitled "The Colours of Eroticism in Ancient Asia," was delivered in the big Green Room of the Philadelphia Arts Centre, an imposing pink brick building topped by the inevitable Stars and Stripes and located on West Independence Boulevard. It was enthusiastically received and warmly applauded. Helen had infused it with just the right proportions of scholarship and humour and with her slight French accent was inimitably charming. The question period was followed by a cocktail party given by the city in the exhibition hall on the third floor (California champagne, white and yellow cheddar, hors d'oeuvres, raisins).

Filing into the exhibition hall, the audience, having just

finished listening to a theoretical discourse, laid eyes on nubile lads and lasses, mountings and sodomizings, blowings and stuffings, the performers artistically displaying their impulses, flaunting their balls, puckering their lips, pulling their penises, caressing their vulvas, wobbling their elegant breasts, parading their flower-decked asses and celestial smiles in luxurious surroundings. Moving from one picture to the next—I'd arranged them in chronological order as Helen had requested—the ladies and gentlemen of Philadephia's genteel set tittered self-consciously, comparing their own rudimentary sexual practices with those of barbaric centuries long gone. The ladies, cheeks delicately rouged, stole curious glances at their neighbours' flies. To the last crumb, those bankers!

This trip was doing me good. It had got me away from the daily round, on an expedition to the civilized frontier; the caterer had thoughtfully provided me with a bottle of Napa Valley mums which I was keeping cool in the moss in an earthenware planter, the home of a luxuriant jade plant. Helen, relaxed and ravishing, strolled from group to group, explaining certain of the paintings, receiving well-deserved compliments. I would have liked her to move about the room on my arm, but she kept her distance, sinuous in a black dress, a long string of pearls about her neck. In a corner, I took a drink of champagne and then put down my glass, raised my head high and stood like a naval officer at attention, hoping to catch her eye, perhaps a smile of complicity. This very night we'd be at the Philadelphia Marriott, together beneath the potted palms.

Champagne gives one wings and in due course Helen used hers to shoo away the intruders, who finally departed, leaving us alone.

"Well, François, if it all goes as well in New York as it has here, we'll have made a place for ourselves in the toughest of

American circuits to break into. I'm bushed."

"Are you happy?"

"Delighted. I couldn't have wished for more. I even called Daddy a little while ago to tell him how well it went. He was dozing beside the phone. Such a generous man!"

"Well, it's past midnight ..."

"And Daddy works too hard. Anyway, I described the situation and he suggests that you spend the night here. He's worried, Philadelphia has a bad reputation. I think they'll be able to find you a camp cot."

"You want me to lock myself up in this room? I don't have any of my things ..." I was distraught. Hadn't slavery been abolished here in this very city?

"I'll send your suitcase over by taxi, the hotel's just round the corner, then you won't have to leave the paintings till they come to take them down tomorrow morning. I'll see you at the airport at one o'clock. It's agreed then?"

"I'd like to know if this is really Monsieur Rosen's idea."

"Of course."

She had already turned away and was about to step through the door when I flung after her, "You know, Helen, I didn't really think I was going to get cozy with the boss, but I did think we might go dancing, to celebrate your success."

She turned back to face me, framed in the doorway; clothed, motionless, she was a thousand time more arousing than all those miniatures put together, and I saw that she had decided to make light of my obvious infatuation. She was sought after day and night, men buzzed like flies or strutted like peacocks around her. There wasn't much future for me in her orbit. What was François Galarneau to her, even with a white cord at his shoulder?

"Daddy's right, you think too much, François. You might have done other things with your life, great things perhaps, but that has nothing to do with me; we need you here tonight."

I was hopelessly in love with a highbrow filly who didn't want to horse around.

"As you wish." And I held my hands on the side seams of my trousers and gave her a little bow.

I had written to Jacques to wish him bon voyage on his trip to Russia and announce to him that his brother, security's Superman, was undertaking a trip of erotic nature with a millionairess whose arms were open wide. But a pillow was all my arms were going to enfold. In France, Jacques had told me, writers often inhabit opulent houses or chateaux with lavish grounds leading to manicured woods of beech and oak. In North America they're more often found in trailers or cubbyholes, cargo planes or cold exhibition halls. And princesses laugh in their faces and sleep in hotels.

48. There weren't many cars outside in the street, of which all I could see was a poorly-lit corner below. An October wind whistled softly at the windows. I stood before one miniature after another in the half darkness, thinking of Helen, who at this hour must be sleeping, naked under a light sheet. I came to a stop in the middle of the room, the floorboards creaking under my feet, put my hand inside my uniform, took hold of my penis and jerked off. In disappointment, jealousy, rage and helplessness, I varnished several third-century-B.C. parchment asses with sperm; you leave what mark on history you can.

I stretched out on the folding bed they'd rolled into a

corner of the room for me and was finally dozing off when the telephone got into the act. Ten past three in the morning by my watch. The ring reverberated through the empty corridors of the Arts Centre, the whole building a sounding box. I didn't move; I confess the thought crossed my mind that it was Helen phoning me in remorse, but I couldn't be a complete fool. In my business we're used to nocturnal calls like this, it's usually just some hungry soul thinking he's got the local pizzeria, or some wino in despair. So nights are punctured with ringing telephones, as the sky is with stars, and there's nothing you can do about it but wait till the black hole of silence returns. But the thing wouldn't shut up. I put on my shoes without even tying the laces and. wrapped myself in a woollen blanket. I must have looked like one of those lost souls who wander about in cold castle keeps in hope a prayer will set them free some day. The phone that was making all that racket was on the second floor, on a wall near the great marble staircase. I lifted the receiver and listened without speaking.

"Is that you, François?"

"Yes ... Who is it?" I couldn't recognize the voice whispering in French.

"You alone in the building?"

"Who are you?"

"Arthur, of course!"

"How did you reach me?"

"By phone."

"Don't be an ass."

"Jacques told me about your trip."

"You were in Moscow?

"Been in New York for a year."

"So you go and call me now, in the middle of the night, in Philadelphia!"

"I couldn't contact you in Montreal, the Mounties are on my tail."

"Can we get together?"

This was all Arthur needed. Ten minutes later I had dressed, splashed cold water on my face from a basin in the public washroom and was bright-eyed and alert. I prudently searched the gallery from top to bottom to make sure I was the only living soul in the building. After neutralizing the alarm system, I opened a basement door on the north side. Arthur arrived shortly after. We hugged, whooping Sioux fashion, punched each other joyfully, talked both at once, there was so damn much to catch up with, so many adventures to tell each other.

"Listen, François, we're going to stick together from now on. And Jacques too. We'll get him to come and join us under the palms, in a country worthy of the Galarneaus—sand, sea, sunshine. You're going to help me find the money for the trip."

"But I've got it already! They paid me five thousand dollars in advance. I haven't spent a cent yet."

"That'll certainly help, but there are bound to be unforeseen expenses. Monsieur Rosen's going to do more than that for us."

It was not hard to do and it all went very quickly. We used razor blades to cut the miniatures out of their frames, after which the forty paintings fitted easily into my suitcase. Even without the frames they were still sumptuous, many painted as medallions or illuminated with tracery in gold or India ink.

We left by the door Arthur had come in by. It was raining now and dawn was breaking between the skyscrapers, but no light was yet reaching the street. I thought to myself that the beautiful Helen would have cause to think over what she had said. I *did* have other things to do with my life than wear a Harry Sécurité uniform.

"You know we could get time under American law for transporting pornographic material?" Arthur said.

We went to the bus station and bought two tickets for Hoboken. "Noboby's going to look for us there."

"Remind me when we get to New York, I want to buy some postcards of the Statue of Liberty. The biggest there are."

49. *Goodbye, Jean-Charles! I've just committed my first crime. I knew how to disarm the Philadelphia Arts Centre alarm because you taught me. A Victronics system. Without know-how you're nobody. After all's said and done, it's because of you I'll be able to finish my novel now. You were right, reading does have an unimpeachable logic of its own. I'm leaving with Arthur to join Jacques, we're going into business together. I'll think of you often. Friendship is precious. Keep yours alive for me. As ever.*

~

Goodbye Joachim! You're a great kid, don't let school make a square of you. It hurts to think I won't ever get to hold your hand again. But you'll grow up and then you'll give your hand to someone littler than you. You're the son I never had. The Galarneaus are moving over to make room for the Soons.

Look after the country, our ancestors worked like horses to make it livable. I'm off to hunt wild animals somewhere else but I'll be careful—you and I learned together to keep our eyes peeled. Life is your oyster, Joachim. My love to you.

~

Goodbye Catherine! I the undersigned, with my brother Arthur Galarneau signing as witness, hereby release you from the marriage vows we exchanged and never consummated. I hope Istvan will make you happy and the two of you will have whatever living space you want. The winter that's on its way is all yours. Your turn to shovel!

~

Goodbye Paulo! You thought I'd be back but that's one bet you've lost. I've dropped out. "Can't let my life rot away this way" goes your favorite song. I've got the message now. From here on I'm playing in life's lottery for myself. I'm leaving responsibility for the family, the economy, the society to you. The Quiet Revolution was our doing. Making it over is your job. You lied to me so you could have your family back with you; now I'm off to be back with mine.

~

Goodbye Monsieur Rosen! You're a lucky man, your wife didn't yield to my advances and now I feel I've been had. You're also a man who's got everything, so I won't apologize for absconding with your collection of two-dimensional amorous frolics. You weren't going to take it with you anyway. And besides, the fruits of your patience are going to keep us out of the poorhouse for quite a while. You've been a good boss, Monsieur Rosen, and I've been a good employee, so we're quits, and I'm sending you back my last uniform in a separate parcel. I've insured it because I want to be certain it gets there so it can gussy up one of your weather cocks. Then you won't forget me.

~

Goodbye Helen! This is my first and last love missive. You appear to be inaccessible for me, yet I believe I would have made you happy. I admired your intellectual work. We would have had beautiful children. I used to imagine us living out our lives side by side, you writing your books on art, me struggling not to lose my memory. Doubtless you loathe me at this juncture because I so brutishly disrupted your plans, but at least that is preferable to contempt. Oh, how I would have loved to smother you with kisses, watch you sleep, take you away from your aged husband!

50. "Pretty damn mushy stuff, that!"

Arthur was reading over my shoulder, he wasn't going to let me get careless and give away any clues as to our whereabouts. We were at La Guardia Airport in a waiting room next to an Italian restaurant where we'd lunched on tripe Roman style, washed down with a Chianti more *populo* than *classico* while we took stock of our lives since we'd been grownup men. Arthur was no longer the sickly little brother everybody had sneered at in school, or the Indian I'd looked on with admiration in Brussels either. Arthur was careworn. His struggles for the benefit of Third World peoples had led him to dubious frontiers. Two deep creases above his nose made him look stern and prematurely old.

The Galarneau lineage that had boarded ship at Lisieux in Lower Normandy three centuries before our time now needed a miracle. Sainte Thérèse, intercede for us! But that poor little nun herself must have been as wrinkled as a forgotten apple; I imagined her in charge of cloud cleanliness in Paradise, sweeping industriously as the dark rain clouds went by, and deaf to our prayers, alas.

With time, even the sun cools. You have to know when to bow out. At our feet, moving this way and that on the tarmac, were aluminum insects from the world over, Thailand and Italy, Holland and Russia, Brazil and Israel. The entire earth was there to give us greeting.

The first call came for passengers departing for Cayenne. Arthur had chosen this destination out of cheek; the thought of fleeing to a place renowned for its former penal colony amused him. But besides, the proximity of the Amazon Basin and Surinam, he said, offered strategic fallback opportunities. It had been agreed that Jacques would join us at the Hotel Montabo, with which Arthur was already acquainted.

The theft of the miniatures had made the headlines in the papers, editorialists had fed on the scabrous nature of the paintings, and there was juicy speculation surrounding my disappearance. Had I been kidnapped by some gang? Murdered and thrown into the Delaware River? Or was I the cunning accomplice of some international machination? Harry Rosen, whose picture appeared on the front page of the *Daily Mirror* with his wife Helen at his side, was entreating the perpetrators of the theft not to do anything hasty, and to make contact with him. Which latter Arthur did with great aplomb from the Iroquois Hotel in New York. Monsieur Rosen, bypassing the encumbrance of police formalities, hastened to buy back his miniatures on the black market. The sum was tidy and enabled us to rectify an historical misdirection: Louis XIV, the Galarneau king, had reigned over both French Guiana and Canada; perchance our ancestors had boarded the wrong ship.

Second call. I tried to look inconspicuous, melt into the

background. Arthur, who was sought by police of every description, was sporting a yellow baseball cap on a "blind the gun dog" theory that had served him well hitherto. But he suddenly said to me out of the corner of his mouth, "We don't know each other. I'm going to fade. Unless we're travelling with a football team, this place stinks of FBI. If I don't get on the plane I'll join you some other way."

I took my place in the queue forming at the counter where an earth-bound flight attendant was checking her passengers' names against her lists. The boarding proceeded slowly and punctiliously and I saw Arthur backing lobster-like out of the Indian file, shedding his shell. His fluorescent baseball cap appeared on the head of a small boy, who took to his heels. My picture had been all over the newspapers, my stomach was in a knot, but no one recognized me; people aren't much interested in victims.

The flight through an azure sky was uneventful, the movie vapid and the food tasteless, and the plane put down softly at Rochambeau Airport. The sea had a brownish cast. It was unusually cloudy for this time of year, the taxi driver told me on the way to the hotel. He was right; since then the sky has cleared, storms are rare and welcome, they drive out the humidity the way one drives off strange dogs. Every day I go and buy a newspaper near the Place des Palmistes. You never know. Arthur might try and get a message to me.

Christmas is coming. How am going to get through the festive season in a forest of rubber trees with the latex running?

I've deposited Monsieur Rosen's money in a branch of the Banque National de Paris near the brothel quarter, where the houses perfume the air with vanilla. I have an idea I want to put to my brothers when they arrive. After all, we're not going to grow nutmeg, pepper or Cacao pineapples. Or turn our bellies to the sun and play Los Galarnos. It's occurred to me we might submit an official request to the French authorities, seeing that only they could help us realize this project. I mean, obviously the engineers at Cape Canaveral could accommodate us between an American shuttle and a Japanese satellite, but we'd have to approach the Pentagon. I'd rather approach the Hexagon; in France they speak our language and for us it's there it all began.

I'd be ready to invest eight hundred thousand dollars in the venture to cover the training of the Galarnauts and the cost of the Great Liftoff. That's almost the whole sum the miniatures brought us. I know Arthur would agree. And if Jacques objects? I'll bring him round with rum and cane syrup, lime, a little sugar and some ice cubes. Because this is our only way out. If the authorities at Kourou will agree to open an interstellar window for us, we'll be the first Québécois since Jacques Cartier to embark on a real voyage, I mean, steer for unknown lands. There's no getting away from it, the one we were born in doesn't belong to us any more.

Geez!